아일랜드 타임 ISLAND TIME

겨울꽃 · 봄꽃 WINTER FLOWER & SPRING FLOWER

아일랜드 타임
-겨울꽃 · 봄꽃

초판 1쇄 인쇄   2012년 3월 22일
초판 1쇄 발행   2012년 3월 29일

지은이 | 이은진
펴낸이 | 손형국
펴낸곳 | (주)에세이퍼블리싱
출판등록 | 2004.12.1(제2011-77호)
주소 | 서울시 금천구 가산동 371-28 우림라이온스밸리 C동101호
홈페이지 | www.book.co.kr
전화번호 | (02)2026-5777
팩스 | (02)2026-5747

ISBN 978-89-6023-779-7 03810

아일랜드 타임 ISLAND TIME

겨울꽃 · 봄꽃 WINTER FLOWER & SPRING FLOWER

이 은 진 EUN JIUN, LEE

책 머리에

한 여행자로서 갈리아노 섬의 초청해 주신 가족들에게 큰 감사를 여기 있는 그림으로 대신(代身)하며, 세계 어느 곳에서든 관심있는 사람 누구에게나 한국화(韓國畵)에 관한 소개(紹介)가 되고, 그 그리는 기술(技術)에 대한 기본적(基本的)인 안내(案內)로써 이 그림책이 활용되기 바라며, 예술사학자 곰브리치(E.H. Gombrich)의 '미술의 역사(The Story of Art)'에서의 도입부(Introduction)의 미술 감상(鑑賞)의 방법에 관한 논지(論旨) 중 마지막 단락(短絡)에 서술(敍述)된,

"예술 작품 감상을 통하여 사람이 마음의 평화를 느끼는 무엇인가에 관하여는 아무런 가르침이 없다 (There is no telling what one might bring home from such a journey)."

라는 맺음말에 따라, 이 책의 독자들이 책장을 넘겨 끝까지 감상하게 될 표현의 한 방법에 의해 각자의 마음의 평화에 가 닿게 되기를 바랍니다.
더불어 본 번역을 교정해 주신 로즈, 앤드류, 제니에게 진심으로 감사드리며, 집필작업에 도움주신 모든 분들께 감사드립니다.

이 은 진

PREFACE

As a guest and traveling artist, I hope these research drawings will give thanks to my hosts on Galiano, I hope my friends will use this drawing book as guiding material when introducing whoever has interest in fine art everywhere in the world to Korean Painting in the basic line, and still wish my readers will 'bring home', by an intuitive way for expression shown through all the pages in this book, citing a point of argument about the way of appreciation of art works which I read in the last paragraph of the introduction part in "The History of Arts" by E. H. Gombrich, as follows.

"There is no telling what one might bring home from such a journey."

Together with that, I should say thank you heartily to Andrew, Rose, Jenni for their proof-reading of my translation into English from Korean, as well as everyone who helped and supported my writing.

Eun Jiun, Lee

목 차

CONTENTS

1장. 겨울 동반(同伴)
Companionship in Winter

조지아 해협의 배가 지나간 자취,
2006년 겨울, 도화지, 수채물감, 35×44Cm^2
Boat Wake in the Strait of Georgia,
Winter 2006, Watercolours, Drawing paper

근 심

페리보트가 달리는 동안 뒤로 밀려가는 해협의 파도거품을 보며, '겨울나기'에 관한 근심이 파도와 함께 바다 깊은 곳으로 가라앉는 듯 하다고 느꼈다. 잇닿는 또 다른 거품을 보며, 겨울에도 영상의 기온이 유지되는 목적지인 갈리아노(Galiano) 섬에서 보내게 될 시간을 그려 보았다. 이 항해는 이미 첫 눈이 내린 캐나다와 미국의 국경 근처, 높은 산 위의 케러메오스(Karamouse) 마을에 있는 첫 번째 초청가족의 집에서 한 달간의 자원봉사를 마친 후, 따뜻한 곳을 찾아 가게 된, 두 번째 초청가족이 있는 곳으로 향한 여로(旅路)였다. 나의 여행은 국제헬퍼교환 프로그램에 의해 시작되었다. 이 프로그램에 가입한 호스트와 게스트는 상호 일손이 필요한 분야에서의 도우미 역할과, 그에 상응하는 숙식과 문화체험의 기회를 교환 제공하여, 게스트에게 호스트의 언어 실습에 도움을 주는 국제 프로그램이다. 이 언어실습을 위한 늦가을 여정(旅情)에는, 캐나다의 가족 성탄절과 섬 생활에 관한 여유있는 기대가 더불어 있었다. 더욱이, 이민국(移民局)에서 나의 그림을 보여주며, "여행 중에 영어를 익히며 나의 그림작업을 할 겁니다!" 라고 말했듯이, 이 프로그램에서 허용하는 자원봉사 성격 내에서, 그림에 관련한 일을 할 수 있기를 꿈꾸었다. 파도를 보며 근심을 하기보다는 희망을 그려 본, 한 시간 가량의 페리 항해는 스털디즈 베이항에서 마무리되었다. 저녁 어둠 속에서 녹색의 나무냄새를 실어오는 신선한 바람을 맞으며 부두를 걸어, 그 끝에 차를 대기하고 기다리시는 초청가족과 함께 집으로 향했다.

11

Concern

The breaking wave spumes of the wake in the Strait of Georgia were pushed back, as a ferry boat I boarded was running onward. This brought on worries about the stay for winter. That is, the waves felt like falling over to sink down onto the deep ocean bed taking my worries. Watching another wave arise, I envisaged the appointed time when I would spend on Galiano, my destination, where it keeps warm above freezing even in winter. This voyage aboard the ferry was to my second host family's place preferable for its warmth, after completing my first volunteer job in a farm house where the first snow had already fallen in a village named Keremeos on a highland near the boundary between Canada and the U.S.A. for a month. The journey of mine was initiated by a program called International Helper Exchange Program. It provides a list of guests and hosts who want to exchange help with their guests from abroad in providing accommodation, which was accompanied by a cultural and practical experience to help the guest with practice of the host's language. Additionally, the serenity in mind of expectations of a Canadian family Christmas and an island life was part of my journey in late fall. Furthermore, I wished to volunteer in a field related to fine arts in the capacity of a volunteer helper as far as the program affords, as I had said "I would like to do my art work through my travel while practising English!" to an immigration officer showing my drawings when I had entered Canada. My voyage during which I envisioned the hopes rather than worried for about an hour finished at Sturdies Bay Harbour. After walking along the pier, in the fresh sea wind scenting the wooded island in the evening darkness, I was picked up home by my host family who had been waiting for me in front of their car.

웰러 베이 근처 작은 곶(串)의 오두막,
2006년 겨울, 도화지, 수채물감, $35 \times 44 \text{Cm}^2$
Cabin on a Cape Adjacent to Whaler Bay,
Winter 2006, Watercolours, Drawing paper

파라다이스

섬 동편의 해협을 따라 놓인 스틱스 알리슨 길에 위치한 집으로 저녁 어둠 속에서 달리는 중, 웰러베이 근처를 지나며 한 여관의 지붕에 세워진 'Paradise' 라고 검게 씌어진 큰 하얀 바탕의 간판이 눈에 띄었다. 조금 더 나아가 나무에 둘러싸여 외로이 서 있는 작은 곶(串) 의 오두막이 눈길을 끌었다. 이튿날 낮 시간에 다시 가서 본 이 집은 오래된 나무의 진갈색을 띠며, 미국 독립전쟁의 근간으로 알려지는 소설 '엉클 톰의 오두막'[1]을 떠올리게 했다. 이 소설에서 캐나다 가족은 노예의 속박으로부터 달아난 흑인을 받아들인다. 그런 흑인들에게는 '캐나다 흑인의 역사'[2] 에서 박사 사무엘 휴(Dr. Samuel G. Howe)의 프리드만 청문회[3]에 제출된 보고서의 한 구절을 인용하여, '인격적 삶' 이 부여된 것으로 시사(示唆)된다.

　　　"---선택된 사람이어서가 아니라, 단지 자유인이기 때문에"

그 앞의 작은 만(灣)에는, 누군가 낚시를 하거나 다른 곶(串)으로 즐겨 노를 저을 듯이 보이는 작은 나무배가 있었다. 저녁 어둠이 짙어지면, 굴뚝으로 뿜어져 나올 연기가 상상되었다. 프로그램을 통해 초청 가족을 만나 추위를 피하게 된 여행자로서의 나의 처지는, 그 흑인 피난민이 처한 상황에 일견 비슷하다고 느꼈다. 집에 도착하자, 차의 헤드라이트에 비춰진 '아일랜드 타임' 이라는 푯말 근처를 거닐던 다섯 마리 가량의 사슴 떼가 멈춰 서서 우리 일행을 마주 보는 것을 보았다. '이 섬은 야생 동물과 인간이 공존하는 낙원이구나!' 라고 여겼다.

Paradise

On our way home toward Sticks Alison Road which runs along the Strait of Georgia, I saw in the evening darkness a sign exhibited on the roof of an inn on whose white background "Paradise" was written in black. It was situated near Whaler Bay. Soon after passing by the bay, my eye was drawn to a cabin standing alone among trees on a small cape. From Sturdies Bay Road at a little distance in the next daytime, I saw an old dark brown cabin giving a look so humble and calm that it suggested an image of "Uncle Tom's Cabin"(1). In this novel known as the background of the American Civil War, I could understand the story of Canadian families who accepted the black refugees who had escaped from the bond of slavery of the U.S.A. The Canadians granted them the right to live in "cultivation of human nature" as is articulated in "Black History"(2), citing the last phrase of a report by Dr. Samuel G. Howe, at Freedman's Inquiry Commission(3) in Boston, as follows.

"---Not because they are picked men but simply because they are free men."

On a little cove in front of the cabin, I saw a tiny wood boat with rows within which someone might enjoy rowing to fish or to make short trips across the cove to other capes. I presumed that smoke would belch from the chimney when the evening darkness gets deep. I, as a foreign traveler, hoped to winter in a warm place sheltering from cold in Canada. In a sense, I felt that I had been confronted with a similar situation to what the black refugees faced but fortunately found my generous host family in the exchange program. Reaching my new home, I saw in our car headlight a herd of about five deer stop their sauntering around a sign that read "Island Time". It seemed like a paradise where mankind and wild creatures coexist in peace.

애완 강아지 타피, 2007년 가을, 모조지, 수채물감, 먹, 19×16Cm^2
Taffy, a Pet, Fall 2007, Watercolours, Drawing paper

또 다른 가족(家族)

또 다른 우리를 반기는 가족은 두 마리의 큰 애완 강아지였다. 이빨로 각각 실내화 한 짝을 문 암캉아지 캐시(Cassey)와 인형을 하나 문 수캉아지 딜런(Dillon)은 꼬리를 힘껏 흔들며 안 쪽으로 우리를 안내했다. 인간 문화에 잘 길들어져 있는 것에 놀라워서 이후로 살펴보게 되었다. 그들은 모든 손님들에게 같은 환영인사를 하고 있었다. 가족들은, "냄새와 소리에 사람보다 훨씬 민감하여 언제나 첫 번째 환영 안내자예요!"라고 설명하였다. 그 집에는 꽃 정원이 있었고, 선명한 색채의 퀼트와 그림, 사진 작품과, 다양한 색채의 사진으로 가득한 책이 많았다. 그 가족은 퀼트 예술가와 사진사인 예술가 가족이었다. 또한 여행객들을 위한 '아일랜드 타임'이라는 오성(五星) 비앤비를 운영하고 있었다. 손님이 없는 겨울의 적적하고 한가로운 섬 생활에서 충직한 애완동물과 창조작업은 잘 어울리는 듯 했다. "섬 생활은 시골 생활과 같아요!"라고 섬생활을 안내하며, 나의 여행담을 청하셨다. "여행은 얼마나 오래걸렸나요?" 자상한 대화를 통해 언어실습을 도와주셨다. "여행길에 어려움은 없었나요?" 나는 대답했다. "서부 캐나다를 가로지른 산에서 섬까지의 멋진 여행이었어요!" 더불어, 집안 내의 예술 작업 어느 분야에서나 참관할 기회를 가졌다. 이따금 두 강아지와 함께 스틱스 알리슨 길을 산책했다. "그만 둬!"라는 내 말을 무시하고, 빗물이 괸 웅덩이가 보이면 '첨벙' 물에 빠져 젖으며 꼬리를 흔들었다. 사람의 말 보다는 주인에게 충실하도록 길든 것으로 보였다. 새 언어를 학습하는 것과 동시에, 나는 애완동물과 사람 가족과의 관계와 그 의사소통에 관심을 갖게 되었다.

Other Family Members

Other family members that welcomed us were a pair of big furry dogs named Cassey, a female and Dillon, a male. Both were wagging their tails in delight respectively grasping a sleeper and a doll between their teeth. They guided me inside. I was observing in amazement at such familiar behavior as humans'. The dogs were giving the same welcome to every guest. My host family explained, "Dogs smell and hear so much faster than humans that they are the first welcoming ushers!" Inside the house, there were clear colours of art works - quilts, paintings and photographs in frames, and books with the richness of colourful photos. Outside the house, there were flower gardens with a fine view of the strait. My host family was an artistic family devoted to quilt art and photography. Additionally, the family ran a home business in tourism for visitors to the island, a 5-star B&B, the "Island Time". The loyal pets and creative works seemed to match well with the time on the island that is isolated and free in winter without so many visitors. She introduced me to the life on the island, "It is like a country life!" She helped my language practice asking in a thoughtfully kind manner a few questions about my travel such that "How long it took?" "Was there any hardship?" I answered, "It was a pleasurable trip from a mountain to an island across Western Canada!" Also, I had opportunities to sit in on every visual field within the household. Sometimes, I took a walk with the dogs on the road. Both looked happy soaking completely themselves in rain puddles ignoring my words "Stop it!" Both seemed to be tamed in loyalty to their owner rather than apprehend the human language. This caused me to get interested in the relationship and communication between pets and their human family.

애완 강아지 기니어스, 2007년 가을, 모조지, 먹, 15×31Cm²
Guinious, a Pet , Fall 2007, Oriental ink, Drawing paper

슈메이너스의 동반(同伴) 애완동물

애완동물과 그들의 인간가족과의 관계와 의사소통에 관심을 갖게 된 그 겨울 이듬 해, 아일랜드 타임 가족의 소개로 그들의 예전 이웃인 캐서린(Catherine)의 집에서 '기니어스' 라는 아픈 수캉아지와 원기 왕성한 '타피' 라는 암캉아지를 돌보며, 이들과 말없는 감성적 의사소통을 체험할 기회를 갖게 되었다. 캐서린은 무릎 수술로 한 달간 입원하여야 했다. 주인이 집을 떠난 동안 두 강아지는 나의 책임 아래에서 하루 한 번씩 마을을 둘러보며 함께 산책(散策)하기를 즐겼다. 그 마을은 벤쿠버 섬 동해안의 '슈메이너스' 라는, 벽화로 잘 알려진 조용하고 작은 마을이었다. 마을을 산책하는 대개의 시간에, 벽화를 감상하고 있는 여행 방문객들을 보았다. 마을 중심가의 건물 외벽이나 사인보드에 제작된 서른 아홉 개의 벽화는 마을의 역사를 주제로 묘사하고 있고, 막대한 크기와 다양한 회화양식에서 장관(壯觀)을 이룬다.[4] 벽화 근처의 벨리 뮤지엄(Valley Museum)은 마을의 유물을 전시하며, 그 리플렛(Leaflet) 으로 관객들의 '마을 역사의 이해' 를 돕는다.[5] 마을 주택의 낮은 담장 너머로 정원의 갖가지 색의 꽃과 할로윈 장식을 볼 수 있었다. 평화로운 시간을 보내며, 두 강아지를 그릴 시간을 가졌다. 기니어스는 산책 후 병에 의한 피로로 깊은 잠이 들었다. 반면, 타피는 선잠이 들었다가 나의 움직임에 따라 따를 태세를 취하여, 굳게 다문 입과 질문하듯 응시하는 눈길로 암캉아지의 야무진 특성을 보이며, 두 앞발로 서곤 하였다. 그것은 동반가족 같은 느낌을 주었다. 두 강아지는 혼자 사는 캐서린에게 훌륭한 가족임이 틀림 없었다. 주인이 돌아왔을 때, 그들은 꼬리를 흔들어 반겼다.

Pet Companions in Chemainus

The next fall after getting interested in the relationship and communication between pets and their human family in Island Time, I got an emotional experience in non-verbal communication with another pair of dogs. The male dog, Guinious was ill and the other female dog, Taffy was healthy and rather energetic. I took care of them for a month while their owner Catherine was hospitalized to undergo a knee surgery. She had been a neighbor of Island Time and moved into a village Chemainus well known for its murals on the east shore of Vancouver Island. During her absence, both dogs enjoyed taking a walk daily under my supervision to look around the village. Most of the time we were looking around, some traveling visitors were enjoying a picturesque view of thirty nine murals. The outdoor murals painted on some signboards or on the exterior walls of buildings around down-town were impressive for their large size and varied styles and techniques. These murals depicted a history of the village(4). The exhibition of holdovers and leaflets in the Valley Museum(5) next to the murals helped the visitors in their inspection of the village history along. In most gardens around living quarters, I saw flowers in variable colours and Halloween decorations beyond their low fences. In such peace, I had time to draw the dogs lying on their sides. While Guinious took a long sleep in fatigue from his sickness after walking, Taffy was still energetic enough to stand up on her two paws when awoke from her nap. She readily followed me with a questioning look and a steady gaze in response to my movement. In the firm attitude of the very female, she was keeping her mouth tightly closed. It gave a feeling of companionship. Both dogs must have been good companions to Catherine who has lived alone. On her return, they happily wagged their tails.

스틱스 알리슨 길 막다른 곳의 집,
2006년 가을, 모조지, 수채물감, 먹, 21×29Cm²
House at the End of Sticks Allison Road,
Fall 2006, Oriental ink & Watercolours, Drawing paper

스틱스 알리슨 길의 외딴 집

그 작은 곳의 오두막을 둘러본 후, 나의 새 집에서 가까운 곳을 산책하여 둘러보기 시작했다. 산책 중에는 자연과 나 자신만을 느낄 수 있었다. 그런 고독(孤獨)을 부여하는 조용한 섬에서의 생활이 충분히 평화로운 '안전(安全)' 속에서 지켜지는지 궁금하였다. 스틱스 알리슨 길의 북쪽으로 나아가다가 막다른 길에서 외벽의 하얀 페인트 색이 벗겨지지 않은 외딴 이층집 한 채를 보았다. 아무런 인기척이 없이 조용하여, 호기심을 갖고 주변을 둘러보게 되었다. 뒷뜰 쪽으로는 섬 공동체 숲지대에 있는 산의 동쪽 기슭 나무 숲이었고, 앞뜰 쪽으로는 스틱스 알리슨 길을 너머 조지아 해협 쪽으로 경사진 비탈 나무 숲이었다. 그 비탈 나무 숲은 이 집의 이 층에서는 보일 것으로 여겨지는 해협의 모습을 가리고, 바다 바람을 약간 막고 있었다. 아일랜드 타임 집으로부터 300m 정도 거리가 있는 이 외딴 집에 전신주(電信柱)로부터 닿는 전기선이 보였다. 편의시설을 갖추고 섬의 어느 곳이든 연락이 가능할 듯한, 앞서 고려해 본 '안전한 고독'의 일면을 보여주었다. 그 집에 사는 가족을 볼 수 있으리라는 상상을 하며, 저녁에 다시 와서 불빛이 보이는가를 확인하겠다고 마음 먹으며 집으로 향했다. 아일랜드 타임 가족에게 "혹시 그 집에 관하여 아는 것이 있으세요?" 하고 질문하였다. "아무런 정보를 갖고 있지 않아요!" 라고 답을 주었다. 섬에서의 '안전한 고독'에 관해 궁금해 하는 나에게, 이 집은 사람들의 시야와 관심으로부터 벗어나, 전망 좋은 자연 속에 위치하여 고요함이 가득하지만, 한편으로는, 인적이 없어 일말(一抹) 호기심을 일으키는, 신비(神祕)의 대상이었다.

23

House in Solitude on Sticks Allison Road

A few days after taking a look around the lonely cabin at the small cape adjacent to Whaler Bay, I commenced looking about the vicinity of my new home. On my walk, I could feel only myself and nature. I wondered if the life in solitude on the island is safe enough to remain peaceful. Going ahead to the north on Sticks Allison Road, there appeared a two storey house standing alone at the end of the road. The white paint on the exterior wall was as clear as if it was recently painted. There was no indication of any people around, hence I went to explore the house with curiosity and enjoyed the isolated view. The backyard view extended to a wood forest on the eastern shore of a mountain in Community Forest Land. The front yard view extended to another wooded slope downwards toward the Strait of Georgia. The slope obstructed the view of and somewhat the wind from the strait. I imagined that the view of the strait might be seen from the second floor of the house but not from the road. I saw an electronic wire from a utility pole reaching this remote house about 300m from my host family's residence. It showed an aspect of "the solitude in safety" which I thought permits a family in the house to maintain communication with people everywhere on the island. With my imagination that I might see the family live in the house, I left there for home intending to return to see if any electric lights are turned on in the evening. I asked my host family, "Do you know anything about the house at the end of the road?" My host family replied, "I don't know anything about the house at all!" This house is located in an ideal place with a good view of nature, but why it was kept out of people's sight was a mystery in which I could understand the idea of "the solitude in the safety" on the island.

스틱스 알리슨 길의 저녁,
2006년 겨울, 도화지, 수채물감, 35×44Cm^2
Evening on Sticks Allison Road,
Winter 2006, Watercolours, Drawing paper

공동체(共同體) 문화

　저녁무렵 그 집에 다시 가 보았을 때에도 아무런 불빛이 보이지 않았다. 흰 달이 뜬 저녁 하늘 아래에서 바다로부터의 산들바람에 얼굴을 씻기며 돌아섰다. 어느 날엔가 그 집에 사는 가족을 볼 것이란 짐작(斟酌)을 하며, 이 집을 '신비의 집' 이라고 이름 붙였다. 이후 스틸디즈 마을로 산책하는 길에, 나의 '안전한 고독' 에 관한 탐사는 계속되었다. 섬의 좁고 긴 지형을 섬 사람들은 '국자(Scoop)모양'에 비유했다. 알려진 바로는, 남북 길이는 27.5 km 이고, 동서로 가장 좁은 폭은 1.6km, 가장 넓은 폭은 6km이다[6]. 각각 가장 좁은 부분은 '자루' 에, 가장 넓은 부분은 '우물' 에 해당하였다. 자루 부분의 유일한 도로인 폴라이어 패스 길을 지날 때, 대개의 운전자들은 걷고 있는 사람들에게 차를 태워주는 친절을 베풀었다. 이 히치하이킹은 섬 사람들사이에서 여행담을 즐겨 나누는 평화로운 정보교류의 시간을 주어, 섬 공동체의 안전을 촉진하는 하위문화의 하나였다. 어느 날, 갈리아노 갈림길에 사는 한 미장공의 배려로 차를 타게 되었을 때, 그 집에 관한 이야기를 듣게 되었다. "그 집에서 새어 나오는 불 빛을 본 적이 있는데, 섬에는 글을 쓰는 등 창조작업을 하는 은거(隱居)예술인들이 많아요!" 그에 따라, 그 신비의 집은 예술가들이 선택할 수 있는 은거지의 하나라고 추정하였다. 날씨에 큰 영향을 받는 좁은 '자루' 지역은 그 해 겨울에 내린 폭설로 일부 전신주가 넘어졌다. 그 회복까지, 일상이 끊기고, 애완동물이 함께 있었던 인내하는 자기성찰의 시간이 주어졌고, 이웃으로부터 안전을 염려하는 전화가 있었다. 섬 사람들은 "이따금 겨울에 폭설이 정전(停電)을 동반해 왔어요!"라고 말했다.

Culture in the Community on the island

There were still no lights in any windows in the evening when I returned. As I turned towards home and enjoyed a cool breeze from the Strait of Georgia, I sensed the subtle darkness at the rise of a pale moon. I named the house "Mystery House" imaging that I might someday see the family who may live in the house. After that evening, my research on "the solitude in the safety" idea continued as I made my way south to Sturdies Bay Village. Islanders likened the narrow and long geography of the island to a "scoop" shape. It is known as 27.5 km in length with the narrowest point being 1.6 km in width and the widest point of 6 km(6). The narrowest point corresponds to the "handle" and the widest point does to the "bowl". Some of their own car drivers were kind enough to give a ride to someone walking on Porlier Pass Road, the only road in the "handle". This peaceful hitch-hiking led to an infra culture boosting the safety of the island's community through exchange of travel stories among those living on the island. One day when given a ride by a kind carpenter who lived on Galiano Way, I heard him say "I saw electronic lights of the house!" He added, "On the island, some artists live and work in retreat to do creative work like writing!" From his story, I speculated that the house would be one of the houses the artists in retreat could choose. In that winter, a snowstorm hit the island so strongly that some of the utility poles fell in the narrow "handle" that is prone to weather change. The isolation granted me a period of time of self-reflection until there was recovery from the outage. While my resolve was being with pets during the cessation of a daily routine, I received a few phone calls from neighbors who were concerned about my safety. The islanders who had given rides to me in the community said, "Once in a while in winter, snowstorms have been accompanied by the power outage!"

2장. 성탄(聖誕) 준비
Preparation for Christmas

아일랜드 타임, 2006년 겨울, 도화지, 수채물감, 먹, 35×44Cm^2
Island Time, Winter 2006, Oriental ink & Watercolours, Drawing paper

성탄 페어 준비

　선례(先例)의 섬의 공동체 생활 속에서 '안전한 고독'에 관한 탐사를 즐기는 동안, 섬에서는 자연보존회(Conservancy)[7] 에 의해 영구(永久) 자연보호구역으로 지정된 몇 곳을 비롯한, 섬 전체에 걸친 자연공원으로서의 보존(保存)과 섬의 자연 역사 탐사와 교육활동이 진행되어 왔으며, 섬 예술가들에 의해, 잦은 미술 전시회를 포함한, 예술창작 활동이 활발한 것을 알게 되었다. 대부분의 섬 사람들이 참가한 섬 공회장에서의 할로윈 파티 이후 성탄 전까지의 한 달여 동안은, 섬 예술가들에게는 성탄절 전 일 주일 동안 개최될 성탄 페어 준비로 바쁜 시기였다. 아일랜드타임 가족은 사진실과 거실 한 컨에 마련된 다양한 색채의 천조각과 장신구로 가득 찬 작업공간에서 성탄 페어를 위한 창조작업을 즐겼다. 그런 어느날, 창 옆 체스 탁자 앞에 앉아 창문을 통하여 조지아 해협을 내다보았다. 늦가을에 건너 오던 중 근심을 하기보다는 희망을 그렸던 시간을 떠올렸다. 겨울이 끝날 때를 고려하며, 겨울 동안의 자유시간에 할 수 있는 어떤 가치 있는 일을 구상해 보았다. 이에 따라 언어 학습을 통한 겨울 나기와 함께, 가족의 관대(款待)한 배려로 여러가지 새로운 시도와 경험에 도전했다. "산책할 때 착용할 장갑을 사용하지 않는 천으로 재봉틀에서 만들 수 있을까요?" "시도해 봐요!" 이따금 재봉틀에서 실습을 하였다. 사진실에서는 나의 여행 중 그린 그림 몇 점을 인쇄하여 성탄카드로 만들었다. "제 그림 몇 점을 인쇄해도 되나요?" "시도해 봐요!" 가족과 동반하여 만나게 되는 섬사람들과의 대화를 즐기며, 조용하고 바쁜 성탄준비 시기를 보냈다.

Preparation for Christmas Fair

While enjoying the mystery conjured up from my imagination when dwelling in this community, I came to know that Galiano Conservancy Association(7) had conserved the environment for ecological and historical qualities, offering outdoor education; some natural heritage sites designated as the areas to be permanently protected were over all the island, and that the island artists had worked actively on their creative tasks and had art shows of their works on the island. A period of more than a month until a week before Christmas after the Halloween party held at the community centre was a busy seasonal period for the island artists to prepare for Christmas Fair. My host family enjoyed working their creative work for the fair in their photo studio and at a work section in the living room full of colourful fabric patches and adornments. When they were at work for the fair, I sat at the chess table next to the windows. I saw the Strait of Georgia over which I had envisioned my hopes rather than worried of the stay for the winter on board the ferry. Looking out the ocean, I considered something what is a valuable work to do in free time till the winter ends. Herein, I tried to challenge to learn in new and different tasks which would enable me to gain a practical experience along practising English, thanks to my host family's favor and generosity. Occasionally I practised sewing on my host family's sewing machine. "Could I use your sewing machine to sew my gloves with your unused fabric patches for taking a walk?" "Surely, you could!" I also made a few prints of hand-drawn cards of my drawings drawn through my travel to prepare for Christmas in their photo studio. "Could I print some of my drawings?" "You could do!" As busy and calm seasonal time passed, I was practising English through conversations with the visitors and islanders I met by accompanying my host family.

퀼트 월례회, 2006년 겨울, 도화지, 수채물감, 먹, 35×44Cm^2
Meeting of Quilt Artists,
Winter 2006, Oriental ink & Watercolours, Drawing paper

예술가 길드 모임

섬 미술가들의 공동 상인(商人)조직인 길드의 하나이자 수업인 퀼트 월례회에 나는 아일랜드 타임 가족에게 동반하여 참석하였다. 섬에서는 문학 정기(定期)모임, 유리, 세라믹 등의 미술 강습, 때로는 애완동물 훈련, 역사 등의 주제 아래에서 비정기 강연회가 있기도 했다. 그 회의는 섬 북쪽 끝에 위치한 숲에 둘러싸인, 이층집에서 개최되었다. 그 집은 그리이스 건축양식에서 보이는 중정(中庭)과 그 바로 위의 지붕 구멍이 계단과 지붕창으로 대치되어 설계되어, 그 지붕 유리창으로부터 들어온 햇볕에 의한 자연 조명이 독특한 분위기를 주었다. 그 곳에서 감각적인 사람들과의 만남과 섬에 관한 이야기를 듣기를 즐겼다. 참가자들은 퀼트 작업을 하며 서로 가르치고 배우며, 성탄페어준비를 위한 안내서를 함께 읽었다. 집안을 둘러보며 그 분들의 모습을 그리는 나에게 관심을 갖고, 내 눈길이 멎는 사물에 관해 자세한 설명을 해주었다. 팔의자 위에 있던, 붉은 귤색과 청록색의 삼각형 조각천들이 각 열을 따라 교차배치되어 그 보색대비가 눈길을 끌던 퀼트쿠션에 대해, 회의장(回議場)은 "일 세기(世紀)를 사신 나의 증조할머니의 작품이에요!" 라고 설명하였다. 녹색과 주황색의 강한 색채대비를 보여주는 깃털 펜에 눈길이 가자, "이 곳에서 멀지 않은 섬 북쪽 끝에 사는 섬의 원주민인 페네라쿠트(Penelakut) 부족 인디언 중 한 예술가의 작품이에요!" 라고 누군가 설명하였다. 그 집을 지은 유럽인의 어떤 물건과 교환된 것으로 미루어 짐작해 보았다. 마침내, "예술가 길드에서 개최하는 '라이프 드로잉' 에 참가해 보세요!" 라고 권하셨고, 아일랜드 타임 가족은 참가비를 지원해 주셨다.

Monthly Meeting of Artists Guild

On a monthly meeting of Quilt Artists, a branch of Artists Guild and one of the art classes that had been held on the island, I accompanied my host family. Other periodical meetings of art included those about glass blowing, ceramics, poetry and so on. Also aperiodic lectures on certain subjects - pet training, history and so forth, were arbitrarily held somewhere as the occasion arose. The meeting was held in a two storey house surrounded by a forest around the north tip. This dwelling was built in a plan in which the courtyard(Atrium) and the roof hall(Compluvium) straight above the atrium that had been shown from the Greek architecture were replaced respectively with a staircase between the ground and second floors and with a set of ceiling glass windows. It naturally illuminated the interior by the sunlight through the ceiling window. There, I enjoyed hearing participants' stories of daily living on the island and meeting the sensitive quilters. They were teaching and learning their techniques one another while working on their patchwork and reading a guide of the preparation for the fair. When paid attention to me who was looking around and drawing them, they gave kind explanations of the artistic items on which my eyes fixed. The chairman explained a quilt cushion on an arm chair, which showed a complementary colour contrast arranged alternately ruddy orange and bluish green cloth patches in triangle shapes. "It is my great grandmother's work!" She added, "She lived for a century!" Someone explained a strongly coloured feather pen, "It was made by an artist in the native Indian population, Penelakut tribe who still live in their community at the north tip near here!" It seemed to be a bartered item with the natives for something of the immigrated European used to build the house. Finally, they told "There is a Life Drawing session by an Artists Guild!" One of them encouraged me, "Why don't you participate in the session?" My host family supported me by paying the entry fee.

애완 고양이, 2006년 겨울, 한지, 먹, 25×35Cm²
Cat, a Pet ,
Winter 2006, Oriental ink & Watercolours, Drawing paper

애완 고양이

　그 집에는 한 집 고양이가 조용히 안밖으로 움직이거나 얌전히 멀리 앉아 있었다. 섬 생활 중 방문했던 몇 집에서 보게 된 고양이들은 강아지와 마찬가지로 사람가족에게 훌륭한 동반이 되었다. 알려진 바로는, 강아지들이 무리를 지어 썰매를 끌 수 있는 반면, 고양이는 개별적으로 조용히 움직인다[8]. 그들 중 일부는 어떤 여행자들에 의해 섬에 남겨졌거나, 야생에서 태어나 숲에서 왔다. 그들의 사람과의 관계를 관찰하며 두 개의 경우로 묶게 되었다. 첫 번째는, 그 회의장소에서 본 고양이처럼, 주인 가족에게 충직하도록 길들었지만 나에게는 낯선 경우이다. 폭설로 인한 정전동안, 추위를 피하여 만화가 어넽 쇼(Annet Show)의 작업실에서 하루 밤을 머물며 본 스무 살의 고양이와, 한 여성 미장공의 집에서 일 주일 동안 꽃정원을 돌보며 본 네 살의 고양이들이 그 예이다. 이들은 온종일 꼼짝 않고 한 곳에 웅크리고 앉아 있다가 주인이 오면 뒤따라 움직였다. 두 번째는 야생 기질을 벗어나 길들어 가는 중이며 나에게 낯이 익어 가던 두 살의 고양이들의 경우이다. 나중에 자원 봉사를 하게 된, 앤드류(Andrew)의 미술관에서 본 고양이와, 그의 소개에 의해 칠 개월 간 돌보게 된 그의 친구 로즈(Rose)의 세 고양이와 한 강아지로 이루어진 애완동물 가족 중, 두 고양이들이 그 예이다. 이 고양이들은 대개의 낮시간 동안 근처 숲에서 뛰어 다녔다. 앤드류의 고양이는 애정으로 주인의 뺨을 핥곤 했다. 로즈의 집에서는 애완 고양이와의 의사소통을 체험하며 그 관찰을 전개했다. 첫 만남에서는 달아났지만, 시간이 지남에 따라 나의 곁에서 신체언어를 사용하여 애정과 요구를 표현하게 되었고, 그 강아지와 고양이의 가족관계가 또한 흥미로웠다.

Cat, a Pet

In the dwelling the quilt meeting was held was a pet cat sitting meekly at a distance or moving in and out. The cats in a few households I visited during my whole stay on the island seemed like good companions of humans as well as the dog pets. Whereas the dogs work in a synchronized task such that they pull a snow sledge, the cats move solitary and silently, according to a known article(8). Some of them were from the wild found abandoned by some travelers or initially born in the wild. Observing their relationship with humans, I grouped them into two cases. In one case of them that were tame in loyalty to their owner but strange to me, such as the cat in the dwelling the quilt meeting was held, I included two cats respectively at the age of twenty and four years. I saw the former at a cartoonist Annet Show's studio when I spent an overnight sheltering from cold during the power outage resulted from the snow storm. The latter with a big white spot on her neck lived in a woman carpenter's home, where I stayed for a week to look after her flower garden. Both of them were sitting somewhere inside the house daytime while nodding off, then followed silently their owner when they came home from work. In the other case of them that were growing tame and on familiar terms with me, I included three two-year-old cats. One of them was in Andrew's home art gallery museum where I volunteered later, and the other two were the members of a pet family of a dog and three cats I looked after at Rose's home for seven months on Andrew's recommendation. All of them enjoyed running around vicinity woods daytime. The cat of Andrew's used to affectionately lick his owner's cheek. At Rose's, I progressed on my observation of the communication between humans and cats and experienced it. As time passed, they got showing their affection and asking for their need at my side using their body language, even though they had been shy to run away at the first. Further, it was interesting to see the relationship between the dog and cats in the pet family.

라이프 드로잉, 2006년 가을, 모조지, 먹, 29×21Cm²
Life Drawing, Fall 2006, Oriental ink, Drawing paper

성탄 페어

아티스트 길드에 의한 라이프 드로잉은 폴라이어 패스 길 동편의
구스 쿡(Goose Cook)이라 불리는 오두막에서 개최되었다. 이 모임은
지도교사가 있어 관심 있는 누구나 참석할 수 있었고, 긴장된 작업 시
간 동안 스스로 배워 완성된 작품들은 전시되어 상호 작업 기법을 교
환할 수 있었다. 또한 성탄 페어를 위한 준비이기도 한 유익한 수업이
었다. 갖가지 도구를 사용하는 서양화법 작품 속에서 나의 붓 터치에
의한 속사화(速寫畵)는 독특하여, 요청에 의해 실기시범을 보이게 되
었다. 나중에 귀국하여 서양화법으로 사물을 그리기를 시도했을 때, 이
수업과 그 분들을 떠올렸다. 소견에서는, 이 예술적 교류는 서로 다른
문화를 가진 사람들이 우호를 다지는 결과로 이끄는 듯 했다. 이 수업
은 성탄 페어 이후, 폭설로 인하여 한동안 중단되었고, 로즈의 집으로
옮긴 후, 나는 '아일랜드 타임' 작업에 집중했지만, 섬에서의 전시회를
계획하고 있는 그 분들의 작업실이나 화랑을 방문하여 대화를 나누기
를 즐겼다. 성탄절 전 일 주일 동안, 약 250 평 규모의 섬 공회장에서
마침내 성탄페어가 개최되어, 예술가들은 자신의 가설대에 작품을 전
시했다. 이 페어는 세계 곳곳으로부터 온 성탄 방문객들로 붐볐다. 대
낮의 눈내린 바깥의 흰색과 대비된 어두운 실내는 퀼트, 회화 작품 등
의 다양한 색채와, 전등 빛에 반사된 세라믹, 유리 등의 소재가 반짝이
며 성탄절의 은총을 경축하는 듯 했다. 나의 부탁에 배려해 주셔서, 초
정가족의 퀼트 전시대 위 한쪽에, 한국화를 소개하는 간략한 표시말을
붙여, 라이프 드로잉에서 그린 남여 한 쌍의 속사화와 여행 중 그렸던
풍경화들을 인쇄한 몇 점의 성탄카드를 전시했다.

Christmas Fair

The life drawing by the Artists Guild was held in a cabin called Goose Cook Cottage situated in the woods east of Porlier Pass Road. It was a practical class on the ground of some merits. First, it was a studio work in which a teacher guided how to draw so that anyone interested in might participate in. Then, there was a display of participants' outcomes worked by learning through a rigid work schedule, accordingly the participants might exchange different techniques of one another. Equally, it was preparation for the fair. There, I willingly demonstrated my croquis with quick brush strokes in oriental ink in response to the participants' request due to its uniqueness different from all of their drawings of the western style in pencils or things else. Later when trying to draw objects in the western watercolour painting style in my country, I recalled this class and them. Inferring from this, it seemed to result in amicability between people in different cultures through an artistic exchange. This class ceased during the late winter because of the snowstorm damage and I had been focused on my drawing project since I had moved into Rose's. However I enjoyed conversations with them who planned to hold their art shows in galleries on the island, on visits to their studios and the galleries. For a week before Christmas, the artists finally held the fair, thus displaying their creative art works on their stands at the community centre as wide a size as about 820 ㎡, where the Christmas visitors from all over the world crowded. In contrast with the white of snow outside daytime, inside the centre was full of various colours of quilts and decoration works, and the glint of glass works, glazed ceramics and the like under the lit electric bulbs which left the inside partly shaded, that seemed to celebrate the grace of Nativity. Out of consideration for the culture exchange, I presented them with a couple of my drawings, a pair of man and woman models drawn through the classes, some prints of my hand-drawn cards, and a brief note for introducing to Korean Painting in a portion of my host family's stand in her favor of my request.

스털디즈 베이 길의 한 쌍의 안내 인형
2006년 겨울, 도화지, 수채물감, 35×44Cm²
A Pair of Doll Ushers on Sturdies Bay Road
Winter 2006, Watercolours, Drawing paper

인간미(人間味)

폴라이어 패스 길과 갈리아노 길의 접점을 벗어나 스털디즈 베이 길로 접어들며, 한 과수원 앞 판매대에 기대어져 있는 사람 어른 만한 남여 한쌍의 인형이 보였다. 폭설이 섬의 일부에 피해를 입히고, 그 여자 인형을 부수고 남자 인형에 약간의 상해를 입히기 전까지, 이 길을 지날 때, 그 한 쌍의 인형을 보는 것을 즐겼다. 두 인형은 웃지 않는 정면(正面)얼굴과 굳게 다문 입술이 표현되어 있어, 노상(路上)의 판매대에 주인이 나오기 전에 안내 역할을 하기에는 상냥하다기 보다는 어색했지만, 인간미가 있었다. 지붕이 있는 판매대는 기둥 윗 부분 가로대에 저울이 걸려져 있었다. 이미 수확기를 지나고, 겨울이 시작되는 무렵이라 아무런 과일이 없었다. 이 길을 지날 때 들리던 강아지 짖는 소리에 로즈는, "저 과수원에서는 강아지 교배(交配)를 해요!" 라고 말해 주었다. 어느 날, 로즈의 강아지 디니(Dini)를 데리고 이 길을 지나가던 때, 과수원으로부터 큰 두 마리의 강아지가 짖으며 뛰어나와 디니를 공격하여 들어 올렸더니, 대신에 들어 올린 나의 장갑 낀 손을 물었다. 이 사건으로 어떤 상처를 입지는 않았지만, 장갑에 구멍이 났다. 이듬해 여름, 다시 이 길을 지나가며 본 판매 과일은 자두였다. 북 쪽에 사는 한 섬사람의 귀가 길에 부쳐, "과수원 주인이 지난번 강아지들의 공격을 사과한다는군요!" 라는 말과 함께 약간의 자두가 나에게 건네졌다. "그 과수원에는 한 학생 자원봉사자가 아이들에게 바이올린 연주를 지도하며 여름 방학을 지내고 있어요!" 라고 섬사람들이 말했다. 왼쪽으로 사라지는 길은 초등학교와 토요일장을 지나 스털디즈 베이 마을로 이르는 길이다.

Humanity

On Sturdies Bay Road turning off the junction of Porlier Pass Road and Galiano Way on my way south to Sturdies Bay Village, I saw a pair of dolls, a female and a male in human adult size. They were leaning their back against the fruit stall in front of an orchard. It was enjoyable to see these dolls when going through the road until the snowstorm damaged some parts of the island. The snow storm broke the female doll and impaired a bit the male doll. They had frontal looks with tightly compressed lips, thereby looking diffident rather than smiling to welcome consumers before a human seller comes out. Despite that, it had showed humanity. A scale hung from the horizontal bar supporting the roof of the stall. However, there was no fruit because it was already late fall after the fruit harvest time and soon winter would begin. One day, Rose and I heard dogs barking, when running along the road together as I was riding in her car she was driving. She told, "The breeding of dogs has been made in the orchard!" On another day later when walking through the road with Dini of Rose's dog to Sturdies Bay Village, two big black dogs ran to us from the orchard and tried to bite Dini. I lifted up him on my gloved hands. At the moment, one of the dogs bit a hand of mine instead of him. Fortunately, I escaped injury in the attack accident, but my gloves were pierced resulting in a little hole with its teeth. The next summer, when passing along this road as usual, I saw the fruits for sale on the stall be plums. Some of the fruits were delivered to me by an islander on his way home toward the north of the island. He passed on, "The orchardist apologies for their dogs' offensive attack on you!" The islanders told, "A college student volunteer is staying in the orchard to tutor the orchard's children how to play the violin during her summer vacation!" The vanishing road to the left leads to Sturdies Bay Village passing by Galiano Elementary School and Saturday Market.

들 고양이, 2006년 겨울, 도화지, 수채물감, 먹, 35×44Cm^2
Cat, a Wild,
Winter 2006, Watercolours & Oriental ink, Drawing paper

잃은 야생 고양이

스틸디즈 베이 마을로의 탐사 길에 그 과수원을 지나 어디선가부터 한 들고양이가 마을 입구까지 나를 따라왔다. 나중에 아일랜드 타임의 가족에게 그 사실을 이야기했더니, "그 고양이를 방에 데려다 키워도 되요!" 라고 하셨다. 안타깝게도, 이후로는 산책 길에 다시 그 고양이를 볼 수 없었고, 대신 나의 잃은 고양이가 되었다. 어쩌면, 이 고양이는 섬의 자연환경보호에 따라 보호 받으며 야생의 사슴, 라쿤 등과 함께 섬 어딘가에서 달리고 있을지도 모른다. 또 다른 섬의 야생동물은 백 오십 여 종이 넘는 것으로 알려진 새였다. 이듬 해 가을 어느 날, 차를 태워주신 분이 하늘을 날으는 새떼를 보며 "섬에는 새 관찰자가 있어요!" 라고 말했다. 그 며칠 후, 벤쿠버 섬으로 장을 보러 가는 길에 차를 태워 준 분이 그 새 관찰자임을 알게 되었다. 새 관찰은 자연을 즐기는 스포츠의 일종으로 알려지며[9], 섬은 매해 기온변화에 따라, 가을에는 따뜻한 곳에서 여름 둥지를 틀려고 북쪽에서 남쪽으로 이동하고, 봄에는 북쪽으로 돌아가는 철새를 이 섬의 이동 길목에서 관찰하는 방문객을 맞았다[10]. 웰러 만을 벗어나는 곳에서 스틸디즈 베이 길을 중심으로 서쪽 언덕에 있는 섬 초등학교의 도서관은 일반에게 인터넷 시설을 개방하고 있다. 그 곳에서 그 분을 다시 만나게 되어 감사의 인사를 하였다. 창 너머로 보인 수업을 받고 있는 아이들은 교통난과 오염문제를 겪지 않는 아름답고 신선한 자연 환경에서 보호되고 교육 받으므로 행복해 보였다. 또한, 그들 중의 한 아동인 로즈의 이웃집 어린이의 경우 같이, 애완동물을 키우며 자연의 법칙과 사회성을 스스로 배울 만큼 총명할 것으로 여겨졌다.

Missing Cat, a Wild

A feral cat had been following me all along till Sturdies Bay Village from somewhere since I had passed the orchard, on my way to Sturdies Bay Village in a few days after reaching the island. Later when I told my host family about the cat, she advised, "You could take it to your room!" Taking her advice, I would look around for the cat appear again on my ways to walk. However, it didn't show up anymore ever after, instead, came to be my missing cat. Presumably, it runs around along with racoons and deer somewhere on the island under the influence of the wildlife habitat conservation. Other species of wildlife than the deer, raccoon, and lost cat on the island were birds over 150 species. Looking up at flocks of birds travel in flight in the sky on a day in the next fall, an islander giving me a ride said, "A bird watcher is on the island!" On my way to Vancouver Island to go shopping on another day after that, another islander who gave me a ride was the bird watcher. The bird-watching is generally known as a recreation for enjoying the wild(9). The island has had the visitors to enjoy watching the birds inhabiting on the island and the other birds migrating from the north in fall and returning to the north in spring at routes(10). When visited the elementary school which stands on a hill west of Sturdies Bay Road just off Whaler Bay and keeps its internet facility open to public, I saw the bird watcher using the internet again. I nodded at him saying "Hello!" from my thanks. The children attending classes who I looked at through the classroom windows were conjectured to be happy, by virtue of being cultured in the beautiful and fresh natural environment and protected from the traffic and pollution. Another my surmise was that they must be clever enough to learn the rule of nature and to cultivate sociability for themselves, as they brought up their pets, seeing as one of the elementary students who was a child of Rose's neighbor brought up her pets.

3장. 성탄 학교
Christmas School

캐브라 갤러리 뮤지엄, 2006년 겨울, 카드보드지, 수채물감,
15×22Cm²
Cabra Gallery Museum, Winter 2006, Watercolours, Cardboard

캐브라 갤러리 뮤지엄

  그 들고양이가 스틸디즈 베이 마을까지 나를 따라오는 동안, 웰러 베이의 남쪽 끝 부근에서 처음으로 눈에 띈 '캐브라 갤러리 뮤지엄' 이라 씌어진 조그만 푯말을 보게 되었다. 그 뒤로 작은 집이 보였다. 그림 관람을 즐기는 나는, 그림을 보기 위해 꽃 정원 사이 작은 길을 지나 그 집으로 다가갔다. '선약하여 문을 엶' 이라는 알림판을 현관 문 위에서 읽고 돌아 서려는 때, 문 위의 작은 창으로 내다보는 사람이 있었다. "지금 약속하고 다음에 보러 오면 되나요?" 하고 물으니, 문을 열며 "들어와요!" 하는 앤드류라는 분을 만나게 되었다. 미술관 안 바닦에는 많은 서류가 흐트러져 있었다. 미술 작품들은 각 방 벽에 걸려 있거나 선반 위에 놓여 있었고, 집의 오래된 흰 벽칠이 벗겨져 나간 얼룩과 뒤섞여 보이는 듯했다. 한 섬 풍경 유화작품은 거실 붙박이장 문 위에 직접 제작되어 있었다. 비디오 테잎, CD 등의 기록자료들이 현관 문 옆 작은 창이 있는 컴퓨터가 있는 방에, 책과 함께 선반 위에 놓여 있었다. 정원에는 이 섬을 발견한 스페인 탐험가 '갈리아노'의 흉상이 보였다. 한 번 둘러 보기만 하기에도 작품이 너무 많아 미술품 집성소 같았다. 그는 일을 하기에는 몸이 허약하고 불편하여 보였다. "이 혼잡을 정리하는 데 도와드릴까요?" 고 제안하며, "저는 이전에 고국에서 미술교사를 한적이 있습니다!" 하고 덧붙였다. "재배치를 해주면 좋겠어요!" 고 선뜻 수락하셨다. 이 후로 온 겨울동안, 시간이 허락하는 한 이 미술관에서 작품 재배치를 하며, 섬 예술가들의 작품을 탐사하고 그로부터 섬 예술가들의 이야기를 듣고, 그들과 직접 인터뷰를 했다. 이 곳은 섬에서 내가 가장 좋아하는 곳이 되었다.

Cabra Gallery Museum

While the cat was still following me till Sturdies Bay Village, I came across a sign which read "Cabra Gallery Museum" in colourful lettering, near the south point of Whaler Bay in Sturdies Bay Village. Beyond the sign, I saw a modest house. Keen to appreciate some art work, I went along a path between flower gardens after passing by the sign. As I drew closer, I spotted a note on the front door reading "Open by Appointment!" and was about to turn back when I saw a person looking out through a little window over the door. "Could I come back later to see the art works if I make an appointment now?" I asked. The person, who I came to know as Andrew, simply pulled open the door and replied "Come in!" There were lots of documents on the floor making messy and art works on the walls and shelves in each room. The art works looked like being mingled with the spots being left behind as the white paint peeled partly off the interior wall. One landscape depicting the island was painted in oil colour directly on the door surface of a cupboard in the living room. Recording materials such as video tapes and CDs were archived on the shelves in a room with two small windows next to the front door where a computer and art books were placed. In the garden outside, a bust of Galiano, the Spainish explorer who discovered an island to name Galiano, was positioned. There were too many art works to even take a look around all at once, thus it gave a feeling of an amalgam. He looked to feel discomfort when moving and too weak to make it tidy. I suggested, "Could I help you tidy up all the messiness?" I added "I was a teacher of fine arts in my country before!" He willingly accepted and made a new suggestion, "Rearrangement is O.K!" During all the winter since then, I had volunteered to rearrange the art works in free time. At the same time, I researched the art works and heard him about the artists who had made the art works, then interviewed with them. This art gallery museum came to be my favorite place on the island.

몬테규 길의 학교버스,
2007년 가을, 카드보드지, 수채물감, 23×30Cm²
School Bus on Montague Road,
Fall 2007, Watercolours, Cardboard

성탄(聖誕) 학교

섬에는 앤드류가 어린이들에게 동화를 들려주는 자원봉사를 하는 초등학교와, '영화와 TV 학교'가 있다. 이듬해 여름, 나는 섬을 재방문하여 그 영화 학교에서 컴퓨터 3차원 동영상 단기과정을 수료했다. 앤드류는 "영화 학교에서 영상예술의 역사를 강의(講義)할 수 있어요!"라고 말하며, 미술에의 관심 뿐만 아니라 영화에의 관심을 들려 주었다. 그는 스페인어를 잘 구사하여 소설 돈키호테(Don Quixote)[11] 연극에서 돈키호테 역을 맡았을 때, 그 인물로 분장하여 찍은 사진이 거실에 있었고, 로즈는 그 사진을 칭찬했다. 어느 맑은 여름 날, 폴라이어패스 길에서 클란튼 길, 몬테규 길, 조오지선 베이 길을 거쳐 스털디즈베이 길의 미술관으로 가는 중, 여름방학을 맞은 초등학교의 버스가 길의 한쪽 비탈에 주차하여 쉬고 있는 것을 보았다. 성탄 새해 주간의 겨울방학이 시작되어, 아일랜드 타임 가족이 손자손녀들의 방문을 기다리고 있던 때에도, 그 버스는 섬 어느 곳에선가 주차하여 쉬고 있었을 것이다. 고상한 즐거움을 위한 성탄절 학교라면, 섬 미술의 역사를 알려주는 교육정보원으로서의 역할이 목적인, 캐브라 갤러리 뮤지엄일 것이다. 관장 앤드류는 갈리아노 섬과 자매 마을인 탐험가 갈리아노의 고향 스페인의 '캐브라시'의 기념식에 초대된 적이 있었다. 그는 성탄절에 청록과 주황색이 대비조합된 성탄 빔 차림으로, 어린이들을 위한 선물을 주머니에 넣어, 준비한 설교를 인쇄하여 교회에 갔다. 그는 수집품들을 '전세계에서 온 영화학교 학생들의 영상, 음악CD 등 기록자료'와 '섬 예술가들에 의한 회화, 공예 등 미술작품', '원주민 미술'로 크게 분류하여 나의 작업을 도와 설명하였다.

Christmas at School Vacation

On the island, there are two schools, Galiano Elementary School, where Andrew volunteers as a story teller and Gulf Islands Film & TV School, where I took a short course, 3D Computer Animation in the next summer by paying a return visit. Andrew showed his interest in film telling me, "I can lecture film history at the film school!" as well as in fine arts. He is also so good at Spanish that acted the character Don Quixote(11) in a play dramatized from the novel at the film school. A photograph of his taken in the character was put on the shelf in the living room of the museum, which was appraised by Rose. On a sunny day during the summer vacation at the elementary school, I saw a yellow school bus parked seemingly taking a rest on a side slope of Montague Road, which links at either end Clanton Road, a branch of Porlier Pass Road, and Georgeson Bay Road leading to Sturdies Bay Road. The bus was presumed to be parked at rest somewhere on the island when my host family members were in snow with longing for their grandchildren's visit from Vancouver at the Christmas holiday. Another school for elegant fun and open at Christmas must be Cabra Gallery Museum that has an educational purpose to provide a source of the island art history by the director Andrew. He had been invited to a ceremony of Cabra City, the explorer Galiano's home town and one of twin cities in Spain with Galiano. At Christmas, he went to church smilingly like Santa, taking his sermon printed readily to read. In the pockets of his Christmas costume with the colour combination of orange and bluish green were full of Christmas gifts for children. His art collections were classified into three categories of the recordings by the students of the film school from all over the world, the art works by the island artists and aboriginal items by the native population by him to help with my rearrangement out.

미스티 판드 카티지, 2006년 겨울, 도화지, 수채물감, 먹, 35×40Cm²
Misty Pond Cottage on Sticks Allison Road,
Winter 2006, Watercolours & Oriental ink, Drawing paper

은빛 성탄의 기다림

　　성탄 며칠 전, 큰 눈이 내린 다음 날 이른 아침, 스틱스 알리슨 길에 나가 보았다. 길 건너 맞은 편 이웃집의 눈 덮인 풍경은 어린 날부터 매 해 보아 온 성탄 그림카드를 떠올리게 했다. 누구의 발자국도 없는 하얀 눈으로 뒤덮인 순수(純粹)의 아름다움 속에 있는 모든 물상은, 멀리서 은종을 울리며 새로 태어날 아기의 탄생을 알려 축복(祝福)을 전하는 천사들을 숨겨 맞고 있는 것 같이 보였다. 조용히 자연에 귀를 기울이면 해협의 파도 소리를 들을 수 있었다. 그 집은 '미스터 판드 카티지' 라는 팻말을 바닥에 꽂고 있었다. 앞 마당 중간에는 자연적인 것으로 보이는 연못이 있고, 뒷 뜰에는 키 큰 사철 침엽수(針葉樹)가 눈에 덮여 있고, 대문 가까이의 헛간 앞에는 새 모양의 큰 나무배가 있었다. 멀리서 보이는 이 집은 행복해 보였지만 역시 호기심을 일으켰다. 정오무렵에, 그 이웃집 부인이 팔에 가득 안길만큼 큰, 부숴진 도자기 조각을 갖고 아일랜드 타임 가족을 방문하여, "혹시 풀 있수?" 하고 물으며, "풀이 있으면 이 부숴진 도자기를 성탄선물로 주겠소!" 라고 했다. 언뜻 보아 그것은 앞 뒤가 맞지 않는 선물 같았으나, 그녀는 뜨개질을 하며 긴 겨울시간을 이웃과 함께 나누는 자애로운 섬사람이었다. "나도 벤쿠버로부터 올 손자 가족을 기다리고 있다오!" 라고 말하며, "섬의 구제점(救濟店)에 가보지 않겠수?" 고 제안하셨다. 구제점에서 오랜 옛날의 수제(手製)장식품들을 보았고, 그녀는 오가는 길에 줄곧 달리는 차 안에서 뜨게질을 하였다. 성탄카드의 그림 같은 은빛 세계에서 성탄절이 다가오는 동안, 이웃과 가족들은 함께 가족파티에 관한 기대를 품었다.

Longing in Snow-White Christmas time

It had been heavy snowy overnight a few days before the Christmas holidays. In the next earlier morning, I went out to Sticks Allison Road to view a snowy view without any footprints. The picturesque view of a neighbouring house covered in the snow across the road made me recall the pictures of the Christmas cards which I had seen at every Christmas. All things in the beauty of purity of the white snow on which no one yet stepped looked like having the angels hidden, that convey the news of a new baby given a birth and the blessings by ringing silver bells at a distance. Attentively listening to nature, I could hear the sound of breaking waves coming from the Strait of Georgia. There, I saw a seemingly natural pond in the front yard of the house, a sign reading "Misty Pond Cottage" and being stuck into the ground, a hut and a bird shape wood boat close to the entrance and tall needle evergreen trees covered in the snow in the back yard. At a distance, the home looked happy, yet I had curiosity. Around noon, an old lady of the neighbouring cottage visited my host family bringing broken ceramic particles as big as an armful of a vase. She inquired of my host family, "Do you have any glue to assemble them back?" She added, "I'll leave these here as a Christmas present for you if you have a glue!" At a glance, it seemed ironic, nevertheless she was a gracious islander who shared with her neighbors the long winter time while knitting. She said, "I'm waiting for my grandchildren family from Vancouver too!" She suggested, "How about going to look around Thrift Shop?" I saw old hand-made decorations in the shop near Bellhouse Provincial Park. All the way while riding in my host family's running car, she was knitting. The Christmas was approaching in the silver ambiance of the snow like the picture of the Christmas cards, while inviting neighbours and families to the expectation of the family time.

조지아 해협이 보이는 뜰에서의 눈썰매 놀이,
2006년 겨울, 도화지, 수채물감, 먹, 35×44Cm²
Snow-Sledging in front of the Strait of Georgia,
Winter 2006, Watercolours & Oriental ink, Drawing paper

손자 손녀(孫子 孫女)

폭설로 페리의 출발이 몇 시간 늦춰졌지만, 마침내 손자손녀 가족이 큰 인사를 하며 도착했다. 어린이들은 애완강아지들과 함께 조지아 해협이 보이는 정원 옆 뜰에서 눈썰매 타기 놀이를 하였다. 겨울 한 중간이었지만 마당 정원에는 봄꽃 식물인 하얀 목련이 활짝 피었다. 공동체 숲지대의 남북으로 뻗은 산을 중심으로 동쪽 또는 서쪽인가, 해변인가 도는 내륙인가, 또한 산 높이가 어떤가에 따라 기온이 서로 달랐다. 서쪽 내륙이 동쪽 해변보다 조금 더 습기가 있었지만 항상 영상의 날씨였다. 아일랜드 타임 가족의 정원에는 동쪽 햇볕이 가득히 쬐이고, 바다바람이 온화한 기온을 만들어 봄꽃이 겨울에도 만개하였다. 어린이들은 가족친지와 애완동물, 선물이 마련되어 있는, 꽃이 핀 온화한 은색의 성탄휴가를 행복해 했다. 그 중 가장 나이가 많은 어린이는 초등 일 년생이었고 일찍 놀이를 끝내고 안으로 돌아 왔다. 그 동생들은 보고 배우는 새로운 어떤 것이든 잘 흡수하고, 성격이 온순한 학령전(學齡前) 나이였고, 오래도록 눈놀이를 하였다. 그 막내는 내가 볼 때 방긋 웃던 삼 개월 된 아기였다. 이듬해 가을, 섬의 코너 스토어의 공고판에서 '도움 필요' 란 공고에 의해, 네 명의 어린이들을 잠깐 돌보는 자원봉사를 하였다. 그 중 섬 초등학교의 일 년생은 책에서 배운 대로 말하는 훌륭한 영어를 구사하였고, 두 명의 유아는 "아니야!"를 연이어 외쳤고, 사 개월된 영아는 약한 '피부 두드러기'를 앓고 있었다. 어린이들과 함께 한 이 감성적 경험은 이 후 캐나다를 세 번째 방문하여 유아와 약자를 돌보는 훈련 과정을 수료하는 것으로 확장(擴張)되어, 사람의 삶의 과정을 좀 더 깊이 이해하게 되었다.

Grandchildren

The heavy snow delayed the ferry departure for hours, however the grandchildren family finally arrived shouting out greetings. The children sledged over the snow with the pets in the yard beside the flower gardens in front of the view of the Strait of Georgia. In the flower gardens, a spring flower Mangolia blossomed at the time in winter. The weather of the island varies depending on whether it is west or east referring to the fiduciary line of a mountain spread along the length of the island in Community Forest Land, whether it is the seaside or inland, and how altitudes of the mountains are. It was a bit wetter in the west inland than in the east seaside, still keeping it over freezing. The east seaside gardens of my host family's house had been suffused with sunbeams and the sea breeze from the strait enough to keep the warmth for the spring flowers to blossom. There, I saw the grandchildren look happy spending the silver Christmas holiday together with their family, pets and prepared presents for them. The oldest child who was a first grader in an elementary school in Vancouver came back in early from the sledging. The preschoolers younger than she were docile and absorptive of whatever were new knowledge to them and sledged long. The youngest grandchild was a baby and smiled when I looked at her. In the next fall, I had an opportunity to volunteer to take care of four children for a while by a note, "Help Needed!" which I read on the notice board of The Corner Store on the island. Of all the children, a first grader in the elementary school on the island was a good English speaker such that he talked as he had learned from books, two toddlers were typical of "no" shouters and a baby had a tiny hardship of heat rashes. This emotional experience of working with the children extended in the course of the caregivers of preschoolers, aged and sick people I took through my third visit to Canada's mainland. The course led me to a better understanding of the processes of human life.

아기의 목욕시간, 2006년 겨울, 도화지, 수채물감, 먹, 35×44Cm²
Baby's Bathing Time,
Winter 2006, Watercolours & Oriental ink, Drawing paper

성탄 절기(節氣)의 근심

마당에서의 눈놀이에서 돌아와, 유리 벽 너머 욕조에서 유리 문을 열어 놓은 채, 아이들은 따뜻한 물로 목욕을 하고, 성탄절을 맞을 준비를 했다. 성탄 쿠키를 나와 함께 굽고, 칲 스낵을 씹으며, 성탄 나무 장식이 되어가는 것을 구경하여 걸어다녔다. 체스판이 있는 거실에서, 할머니는 아들과 함께 성탄나무를 장식하며, "가장 높은 별은 신성한 어린 생명을 상징하는 핵심적인 장식이야!"라고 설명하였다. 아이들은 모두 이 세상에 태어난지 얼마 되지 않는 순수한 천사같은 존재였다. 밤이 깊어가면서 온 가족은 낮에 아들이 패어 놓은 장작(長斫)이 타는 벽난로 옆에서 TV를 보았다. 창문 너머로 그들이 건너 온 어두운 짙푸른 해협이 보였다. 동화(童話)의 용어로는, 산타가 그 바다를 무사히 건너 섬의 어린이들 집에 도착하도록, 바람이 잔잔할지 근심하여 나는 내다보곤 했다. TV 뉴스에서는 "성탄휴가 동안 폭설이 예상됩니다!" 라는 폭설 주의보가 발표되었다. 할아버지와 아들은 전원공급이 안될 경우에 대비하여 가정용 발전기를 가동(稼動)할 준비를 하였다. 할머니는 세계 곳곳의 가족 친지와 친구에게 보낼 한 다발의 성탄카드에 인사말을 쓰셨고, 손자손녀들을 위한 퀼트이불을 준비하셨다. 오후에는 마을 교회에서 운영하는 식료품 배급창고로 성탄절에 불우(不遇)한 이웃과 나눌 저장식품을 가져가셨다. 날씨변화에 민감한 애완동물들이 행복했으므로, 그다지 심각한 재난(災難)은 없으리라고 보였지만, 아들 가족은 무슨 일이 일어나고 있나 둘러보러, 차를 몰아 스털디즈 베이 마을로 갔다. 그들은 비상 식품 등을 사서 돌아왔다.

Concerns in Christmas Time

After taking a warm bath in the bathtub in the bathroom with the glass wall and door kept open, as soon as coming back in from their sledging outside, the children were ready to spend the time of Christmas family reunion in happiness. They made Christmas cookies together with me, munched chip snacks and walked around inside while watching the Christmas tree getting decorated by their grandmother and her son. The grandmother told, "The highest star is the most important part of the decoration, which symbolizes the holly life to be born!" while decorating the Christmas tree in the living room, where the chess board was placed. Every child is regarded as the pure being born in the recent past like an angel. As it got dark, all the family members watched TV around the fireplace where the firewood that was chopped in the afternoon by the son were burning. Through the windows, I looked out the Strait of Georgia across which they had come is in deep blue. I was in doubt if the wind would be calm enough, in the language of a children's story, to the extent for Santa to reach the children's home over the ocean. The weather forecast on the TV announced, "Some snowstorms are anticipated during Christmas Holidays!" The grandfather and his son prepared to operate a home electric generator in case of that power is off. The grandmother wrote to her family, relatives and friends over the world a bundle of Christmas greeting cards and prepared her hand-made quilt sheets for the children. In the afternoon she gave of some convenience foods to share with someone who need them to the Food Bank that has been running by St. Margaret of Scotland Church on the island. Given the fact of that the pets with a keen sensitivity to nature were happy, it didn't look like any potential hazards of snowstorm. However, the son's family had gone out by car to look around down-town to see what had been going on. They came back bringing some food bought at groceries.

중조(曾祖) 할머니의 퀼트 쿠션,
2006년 겨울, 도화지, 수채물감, 먹, 35×44Cm²
Quilt Cushion by Great Grandmother,
Winter 2006, Watercolours & Oriental ink, Drawing paper

성탄 이야기

　성탄 가족시간을 그리면, 그 증조할머니의 퀼트쿠션이 떠오른다. 섬의 어린이들은 불이 지펴진 벽난로 앞 팔의자에서 그런 쿠션에 기대어 오랜 옛날부터 전해져 온 성탄 이야기와 섬에서의 댄스파티 이야기를 들을 것 같다. 이 성탄댄스는 이 섬에 살고 있는 화가 케이트 홀름(Keith Holem)[12]에 의해 제작된, 불이 활활 지펴진 벽난로 앞에서 어린이들과 함께 손을 잡고 둥근 원을 만들며, 한쪽 발을 들어 올려 춤추는 산타를 묘사한 유화작품에서 비롯된다. 인터넷 정보[13]에 따르면 산타 클라우스라는 인물은 자신의 모든 재산을 나라를 여행하며 불쌍한 사람들에게 나누어 준 박애주의적 행동으로 칭송되며, 어린이와 뱃 사람들의 수호성인(守護聖人)으로서 여전히 긍정적 평판을 받는다. 이 그림의 산타는 아무런 짐 없이 어린이와 함께 춤을 즐기고 있다. 활활 타는 붉은 불빛에 의해 던져진 그림자의 춤추는 율동미(律動美)는 실감(實感)을 북돋우며, 독특한 상상적 이미지로 d 애호(愛好)되는 이 그림은 마을 공동체에 의해 구매되어 섬 공회장 벽에 걸려있었다. 성탄 가족시간에 관한 나의 이야기라면, 어린 시절 아버지께서 마당의 큰 전나무에 꼬마 전구선 장식을 둘러 그 날의 은총을 전하신 기억에서 비롯된다. 그 전나무가 공해가 심한 공장지대로 공기정화를 위해 팔려가며 중단되었다가, 당시 전나무와 어린이들과의 성탄과 더불어 다시 기억되었다. 상상을 구현한 이 그림에서 느낀대로 말하자면, 성탄 이야기란, 매해 성탄에 산타의 것 같은 상상의 보따리로부터 새로 생겨 나오는, 어린 날 어른들로부터 전해 받은 끝없는 이야기인, 어떤 것인 듯 하다.

Stories of Christmas

Conceiving of a Christmas Eve with family, I recall the quilt cushion descended from the great grandmother. Any children are presupposed to listen to their grandmother's Christmas stories that had been handed down for generation from the old age and a dance party on Galiano while leaning on their back against such a cushion in an arm chair near the fireplace at home. This Christmas-dancing idea is originated in an oil painting by Keith Holms(12) who lives on Galiano, that depicted an image of dancing Santa by lifting his foot up in a circle by holding his hands with children in front of a fireplace in which the fire wood is ablaze. According to an article about Santa Clause(13), he had been admired for his piety and kindness as he had given away all his inherited wealth to the poor and sick and traveled over countryside helping the poor, herein had become an icon as a protector of children and sailors and still has a positive reputation. In this painting, he enjoys dancing with children without any burden of his gift sack. The painting exalts a sense of reality by a rhythmic movement of the dancing shadow cast on the floor under the blazing firelight in bright orange and red colors, and is loved for its unique imagination. This painting was purchased by the community camber of commerce and hung on the wall of the community centre at the Christmas holidays. As for the Christmas family time of mine coming in mind, it had begun in my childhood until the teenage years when my father had decorated a tall pine tree in my family garden with a garland of electric twinkle lights on a Christmas Eve. Since then, when the pine tree was sold out to a polluted factory plantation to refresh air, my Christmas memory had been deemed to be simultaneously taken away. Then, at the time when being with the children and pine trees, I came to recollect the Christmas memory. In the allegorical term of the unique imagination this painting depicted, a Christmas story is regarded as something what newly comes out of an imaginary sack like the Santa's at every Christmas, that is an ongoing story descended from their seniors in one's childhood.

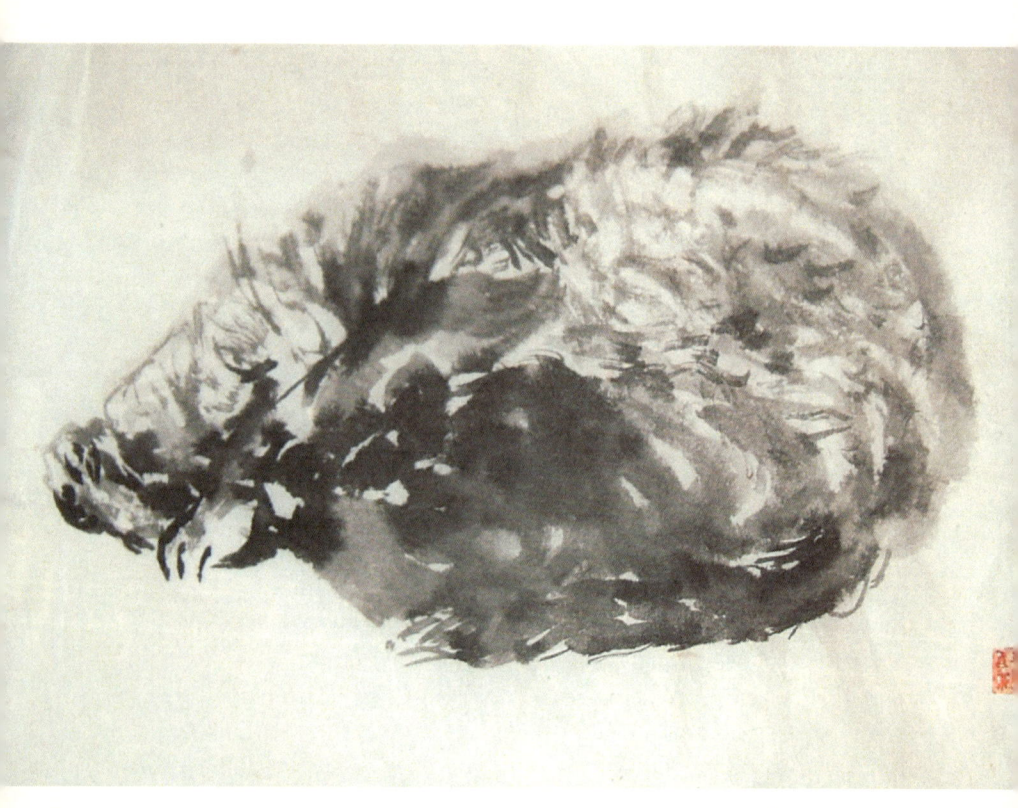

어우러져 가는 고양이, 2006년 겨울, 한지, 먹, 30×35Cm²
Cat Growing Tame,
Winter 2006, Oriental ink, Han(Korean) paper

성탄의 은총(恩寵)

성탄절은 애완동물 가족에게도 은총의 시간이었다. 그림 안의 고양이 비니는 로즈에 의해 그녀의 자매가 살고 있는 밴쿠버 섬 빅토리아의 숲에서 발견되어 데려져 왔다. 녀석에게는 여전히 야생의 성격이 남아 있었다. 낮에는 근처 숲에서 야생 기질을 쏟아내며 뛰어 다녔고, 이따금 로즈의 유일한 암코양이인 또래의 리틀 걸 캣을 위협하기도 했다. 밤에는 디니, 리틀 걸 캣, 그리고 다른 한 고양이가 더 있는 애완동물가족의 집에 돌아와, 식사차례를 지켜 허기를 채우고, 가족에게 애정을 표현하는 듯한 자세를 취하여, 틀어놓은 TV와 DVD의 성탄절 영화를 가족과 함께 즐겼다. 이듬해 여름, 비니는 로즈에 의해, 애완용 상자에 실려 페리를 타고 외과수술을 받기 위해 이틀 동안의 빅토리아로의 여행을 다녀왔다. 바로 그 다음, 로즈는 학업을 위하여 집을 떠나고 나는 그들을 돌보게 되었다. 그 때, 침실로 향하는 좁은 통로에서 마주보고 걷던 비니와 디니 사이에 잠깐 동안의 평화를 깨는 야생적인 싸움이 일어났다. 부상이 없었고, 이후 다시 그런 다툼은 일어나지 않았다. 로즈가 돌아왔을 때, 이 사건을 말하니, "외과수술 후의 애완동물의 신경학(神經學)적인 문제에요!" 라고 설명하였다. '밤에 채소를 서리하던 야생노루의 버릇' 에 대해 케러메오스 마을의 초청 가족이 내린 '자리 싸움' 이란 해석을 떠올려 연관지어 보았다. 다툼의 원인이 무엇이었든, 그 후 평화로운 가족 시간의 은총은 회복되었다. 어느날 저녁, 나는 성탄절을 위한 나의 애니메이션의 음악에 따라, 비니와 다른 애완동물가족과 함께 그 그림 속의 산타와 어린이들처럼 손을 잡고 둥근 원을 만들도록 이끌어 춤추었다.

Grace at Christmas

The Christmas was still a blessed time to the pet family of Rose's. The pet cat Vini in my drawing had been taken by Rose to her home from Victoria on Vancouver Island, where her younger sister had lived, when she had visited her. I took care of him with other pets at her home. He still showed the nature of a wild life. He ran around in the vicinity of home letting off his wild nature daytime. From time to time, he threatened an only female cat, Little Girl Cat in his peer age of the pet family members at Rose's. At night, he came home where a two-year-old dog, Dini, Little Girl Cat and one more cat were living together, and satisfied his hunger in line of their meal turn. Then he would enjoy watching the TV and Christmas DVD I turned on, in a posture seemingly expressing affection to his family. One day in the next summer, he came back home from a trip taking a couple of days by being carried in his cage on the ferry to undergo surgery in Victoria. Soon after returning home, Rose left for her study, thus leaving us alone. Then a wild fight occurred between Vini and Dini breaking peace when both were strolling around facing each other in the narrow corridor to the bedroom with the windows which hung high on the wall. Neither one had got any injuries nor the fight had been repeated since then. I told Rose about the fight later when she returned home. She surmised, "It seems to be caused by the pet's psychological problem after undergoing in surgery!" I even associated the fight to the host family's judgment in Karameous, an "occupancy power struggle" on the wild deer's behavior that had stolen vegetables from their farm at night. Whichever it had been caused by, as time passed, the peaceful time of the pet family was recovered into the state of grace. One evening, I led Vini and the other pets all to dance together to the Christmas music of my animation, holding my hands and their paws one another in a circle like the dancing Santa and children in the oil painting precedent.

4장. 겨울꽃과 봄꽃
Winter Flower and Spring Flower

눈 속에서 싱싱한 잉글리쉬 열대식물,
2006년 겨울, 도화지, 수채물감, 먹, 35×44Cm²
English Tropical Plant Flourishing in Snow,
Winter 2006, Watercolours & Oriental ink, Drawing paper

화가(畵家) 로즈의 집

성탄 며칠 전, 정원의 열대식물이 눈 속에서도 싱싱해 보이는 아일랜드타임 가족의 집을 떠나 앤드류의 추천으로 로즈의 집으로 향했다. 미술에 있는 나의 관심을 지원하여 초청해 주시고 나의 추천인이 되어주신 관대함에 큰 감사를 되돌려 드릴 의무감을 느꼈다. 로즈는 예술가이자 간호사이고 수녀였고, 노바스코셔에서의 학업 동안, 그녀의 애완동물과 정원이 있는 집을 보살펴 줄 사람이 필요했다. 로즈의 집은 폴라이어 패스 길 동편에 위치한, 앞마당의 꽃정원을 둘러 지나가면 보이는 통나무집이었다. 로즈의 집에 도착하여 그림카드로 성탄선물을 대신하며, "여기 머무는 동안 애완동물을 돌보며, 성탄 카드용 그림 작업을 하고, 앤드류의 집에서 자원봉사를 할 거에요!" 라고 하였다. 현관문을 중심으로 양쪽 벽 윗쪽이 유리창이었다. 그 중 한쪽은, 그녀의 설명에 의하면 한 교통사고에서 구해진, 부쉬진 색 유리 조각들을 밖으로 돌출한 투명한 무색의 유리창에 덧붙여 제작한, 갈색 줄기, 녹색 나뭇잎의 나무와 보라색 산들바람을 묘사한 스테인드 글라스 작품이었다. 그 앞 선반에는, 하얀 종이점토로 만든 동화(童話) 속의 성이 놓여 있었다. 하얀 성에 떨어지는 색유리를 통과하며 생긴 그림자와, 색유리로 묘사된 풍경이 창 밖의 나무와 하늘이 보이는 정원 풍경과 중첩되어, 유리의 투명함에 의해 자연 조명을 강조하고 있었다. 로즈의 또 다른 미술작품은 앤드류의 미술관에 있는 유화풍경이다. 녹색 자연 한 중간의 나뭇가지에 걸린 하얀 비닐 봉지를 묘사하여, "오드리 토마스(Audrey Thomas)[10] 같이 국제적으로 저명(著名)한 작가의 집 앞에 여행객들이 쓰레기를 버리고 가요!" 라고 지적(指摘)하던, 자연보호를 주장하는 주제를 담고 있다.

Home of an Artist, Rose

A few days before Christmas while English Tropical Plants were still thriving on outside in the snow, I left the lovable garden of Island Time for Rose's pet home on Andrew's recommendation. I felt a duty to return my host family's generosity; they had invited me in support of my interest in art, and became one of my referees. Rose was a nurse, nun and artist in need of help with her pets, house and flower gardens, while she studied in Nova Scotia. Circling half a flower garden in the middle of the front yard, I came to Rose's log cabin located in the woods east of Porlier Pass Road. Arriving at her home, I gave her the print of my hand-drawn cards as a Christmas gift and explained, "I would like to work on my drawing for Christmas cards and volunteer in Andrew's museum while looking after your pets during my stay in here!" Large windows hung on the upper part of the walls either side of the front door. One side was a bay window of three pieces and a stained glass work over it caught my eye. It depicted a few trees with brown trunks, green leaves and a violet breeze and was created in a way of sticking coloured glass fragments; which were the remnants of a car accident according to her explanation, onto the transparent window. On the bay shelf in front of the stained glass, I saw a white paper clay castle depicting a children's fairy tale. It spectacularly enhanced the natural lighting with the transparency of the glass. That is, the sunshine through the coloured pieces of the stained glass threw light and partly colour shade onto the castle and the scene of trees and breeze was mixed with the view of the gardens outside the window. Another item of her art works was an oil painting hung on the wall of Andrew's museum. It depicted a plastic bag hung down from a tree branch in the freshness of nature branding that "Nature should be kept fresh!"; she explained, "Some visitors to Galiano have thrown their rubbish away in front of the home of Audrey Thomas(14), an internationally acclaimed writer!"

집 고양이 핍스, 2010년 여름, 도화지, 수채물감, 30×22Cm²
Peeps, a Pet Born in a Human Household,
Summer 2010, Watercolours, Drawing paper

박애(博愛) 교육

　　로즈는 박애주의자였다. 들에서 비니와, 리틀 걸 캣을 데려오고, 턱이 나와 늘 아랫니를 보이는 두 살의 디니를 애견가게에서 입양했다. 정원에는 들새들을 위해 물과 씨앗을 그릇에 담아 두어 자주 지저귀는 새 소리를 들을 수 있었다. 주인에게서 박애주의를 배운 애완동물은 같은 뜻을 전하고 있었다. 로즈의 다른 한 애완동물은 유일하게 그녀의 집에서 태어난 고양이인 열 여덟살의 핖스였다. 핖스는 로즈의 긴 여행 동안 돌볼 사람이 없을 때 병에 걸렸고, 살아남기 위해 동물병원에서 한쪽 눈을 잃어야 했다. 처음에는 섬찟했지만, 시간이 지남에 따라 그 버릇이 다른 애완동물에 비해 인간의 행동에 훨씬 다가서 있고, 야생기질을 완전히 잃은 친근함을 느끼게 되었다. 실내에 머물며 조용히 걷고, 집 울타리 밖에 나가지 않았다. 하품을 할 때는 하얀 이빨이 늘어선 분홍색 입안을 보여 주었다. 나에게의 표현은 외로움을 느끼는 아기와 같았다. 밤에 벽난로 옆의 제 보금자리를 두고, 내 방의 문을 긁어 함께 있기를 청했다. 다른 동물가족에게는 엄마와 같았다. 애정을 표현하는 비니를 두 앞발로 덮어 품었다. 어느 오후, 주인의 전화번호가 새겨진 목띠를 두른 고양이가 열어 놓은 앞 문으로 뛰어 들어와, 그 주인이 데려가기를 기다리게 되었다. 그 때, 비니와 디니가 다투었던 복도의 창을 통해 옆뜰에 있던 자애로운 호스트 같은 핖스를 보았다. 로즈와 내가 하듯이, 핖스는 비니, 리틀 걸 캣, 그 길 잃은 고양이와 함께 둘러앉아 앞발로 코를 건드리며 부드러운 야옹소리를 내어, 환영과 의논을 오래도록 하는 듯 했다. 로즈는 "리틀걸캣과 디니가 처음 왔을 때에도 그렇게 환영했어요!"라고 말했다.

Philanthropy Education

Rose is a philanthropist. She took home the feral cats, Vini and Little Girl Cat and adopted a dog Dini from a pet shop, whose chin protruded so far that his lower teeth always showed. Also, I often heard wild birds singing around a water bowel and the seed cases prepared in her flower garden. The pets' behavior spread the same message as the philanthropy learned from their owner. Of all her pets, eighteen-year-old Peeps was the only cat born in her house. Peeps lost an eye of his permanently for life in surgery to a disease he had caught in Rose's absence during a long trip. It looked scary at the first, but as time passed, I observed him behaving in a way that was much more human than the other pets and felt him completely losing his wild nature if indeed he ever had one. Most of the time, he walked around silently, stayed inside without going out over the fence, and exposed the pink of his mouth surrounded by white teeth when yawning. He was like a child feeling lonely to me, seeing his expression of scratching my closed bedroom door asking to be with me after leaving his mat at night. Meanwhile, he was like a mother to the other pets, gently hugging the affectionate Vini with his two paws. One afternoon, a lost cat wearing a collar with his owner's telephone number on it ran into our home through the front door kept open and I came to wait for the cat owner to take him back. Then, through the window in the corridor where Vini and Dini had fought, I observed another habit of Peeps that made him seem like a benevolent host. Peeps was sitting with Little Girl Cat, Vini and the lost cat facing one another in a circle in the side yard. He seemed to be welcoming the lost cat and discussing something with the other cats, as Rose and I had done, by gently touching his nose to his two paws and mewing. Rose told me, "Peeps had welcomed Dini, Vini, and Little Girl Cat in the same way!"

크리스마스 선인장, 2006년 겨울, 중국지, 수채물감, 먹, 18×26Cm²
Christmas Cactus,
Winter 2006, Watercolours & Oriental ink, Chinese paper

겨울꽃과 봄꽃

　　로즈의 집에서 맞은 성탄 무렵의 눈 내린 어느 날, 거실의 성탄 선인장이 피어 이 주일 동안 지탱하였다. 붉은 주황의 꽃잎과 청록색 줄기의 대비는 추운 고난의 계절에 아직 봄을 기다리고 있을 어떤 봄꽃의 생존(生存)의 고통을 상기시켰다. 로즈의 책장에는 화려한 색채의 그림책보다 글이 가득한 책이 많았다. 책은 추운 고통으로부터 살아나온 만개(滿發)한 꽃과 같이 여겨졌다. 어느 날, 앤드류는 로열 브리티쉬 콜럼비아 박물관으로 안내해 주어, 캐브라 미술관에서 본 양식과 동일한 원주민 미술을 그 곳에서 보았다. 섬으로 돌아오는 항구가 있는 시드니에서는 큰 서점에서 서른 여덟 살 된 자신의 애완강아지에 관한 이야기를 담은 책을 보았다. 페리가 섬에 도착하여 사람과 차가 배에서 내리기 전, 큰 철문이 열릴 때, 어둠을 쪼개며 서서히 들어오는 차가운 공기와 빛줄기는 인상적이었다. 다른 날은 벤쿠버 아트갤러리를 방문하여, 전시된 고금(古今)의 미술작품을 보았고, 큰 쇼핑몰과 문구사에서 장을 보았다. 어느 일요일은 교회예배에 참석했다. 대개는 캐브라미술관에서 웹(Web) 미술관(Cablelan.net/cabra)을 무료 도메인(Domain)으로 만들고, 그 곳에 작품 분류 중 앤드류로부터 듣게 된 섬 미술가들의 작업실을 찾아가 그들과 이야기를 나눈 기록(記錄)을 올렸다. 로즈에게 자주 안부편지를 썼다. 애완동물과 함께 한 섬 생활 중 보았던, 기억에 남는 대상을 그리던 작업(作業)을 그녀가 돌아오기 전까지 계속했다. '겨울나기' 로부터 가치로운 일을 구상하여, 겨울을 견딘 봄꽃을 피우듯이, 이른 봄의 그림 전시회를 계획했다.

Winter Flower and Spring Flower

The Christmas Cactus bloomed on a snowy morning around Christmas time and continued to bloom in the morning and to be gone in the evening for two weeks in the first half of my stay at Rose's. The contrast of flowers and stems respectively in orange and green reminded me of the hardship of spring-flowering plants that must survive winter cold till the warmth brings about their bloom. The books on Rose's shelves were filled with writing rather than colourful pictures. The books seemed like the flowers that had bloomed after enduring winter. One day, Andrew guided me to the Royal British Columbia Museum in Victoria, where I saw aboriginal arts by First Nation's artists in the same style as those hanging in the Cabra Gallery Museum. On our way home, in a large bookshop in Sidney near the harbor, I saw a book about a 38-year-old pet dog, written by his owner. When our ferry reached its destination, it was impressive to feel the fresh air and to see the rays of the sun or electric lights crack through the darkness, as the large iron door to the cargo deck of the ferry we had been aboard gradually opened, and people and cars exited after getting in line in the gloom. Another day Andrew accompanied me to the Vancouver Art Gallery where I saw some classical and modern art, and I also went shopping in big shopping malls and a stationary store in Vancouver. One Sunday, I participated in the Sunday Service at the church on the island. However, I spent most of my time at Andrew's museum rearranging the art works, opening a web site at a free domain(Cablelan.net/cabra) and loading up reports of my interviews with the island artists introduced by Andrew, whose art works I had found during my rearrangements and whose studios I visited. Often I wrote letters to Rose, telling her how we were doing. Still, I had continued to draw memorable objects which I had seen while spending my time with the pets, until the spring when she came back home. I planned to hold an art show in spring for pursuing a valuable work - the flowering, in the stay during the winter, on my drawing project.

조지아 해협, 2006년 겨울, 도화지, 수채물감, 먹, 35×44Cm²
The Strait of Georgia,
Winter 2006, Watercolours & Oriental ink, Drawing paper

봄 전시회(展示會)와 새 계획(計劃)

조지아 해협의 회빛 암석이 연녹색을 띤 나뭇잎과 함께 봄볕에 반짝이던 무렵, 캐브라 미술관에서 로즈의 집으로 가는 길에 영화 학교의 학장 조오지(George)의 배려로 차를 타게 되었다. 그의 안내로, 학교에 나의 관심 과정이 개설되어 있음을 알게 되어, 다시 캐나다를 방문하여 수학할 계획을 갖게 되었다. 몇 개월 후 초여름, 로즈의 집으로 돌아가 그녀의 집에서 가까운 그 학교에 다니며 그 과정에서 동영상을 만들었고, 애완동물을 돌보며, 캐브라 미술관에서 자원봉사를 하였다. 섬에서 지낸 첫 해 겨울에는, 로즈가 떠나기 전 성탄 전야에, 앤드류의 집 거실 탁자에서 따뜻한 차를 함께 나누는 짧은 송별회를 가졌다. 두 사람은 앤드류의 돈키호테로 분장(扮裝)한 사진과, 벽에 있던 로즈의 자연보호를 주장하는 유화작품, 나의 그림카드와 두 사람 사이의 우정과 믿음이 빚어 낸 나의 의무에 대해 이야기했다. 성탄의 은총을 느꼈던 오붓한 시간이었다. 두 사람과 아일랜드 타임 가족, 모든 섬 사람들에게 섬 생활에서 주신 도움에 대해 감사를 표현하기 위해, 섬 공동체의 월간 소식지에 '상록(常綠)의 갈리아노' 란 주제로, 캐브라 미술관에서 겨우내 해 온 나의 작품의 전시회가 있음을 알리는 감사의 글을 투고(投稿)했다. 나의 그림 전시회는 연두빛 새싹의 나뭇잎이 돋고 붉은 색, 노란 색 등의 꽃이 핀 이른 봄에 이 주일 동안 이루어졌다. 드문 손님을 기다렸지만, 감사를 표현할 수 있어 행복했다. 아일랜드 타임 가족께서 그 이웃 분과 함께 방문하였을 때, 인쇄된 그림카드로 감사를 대신했다. 마찬가지로, 모든 그림은 인쇄된 그림카드 형태로, 캐브라 미술관에 남겨졌다.

Art Show in Spring and a New Plan

Just as the natural grey rock of the Strait of Georgia began to glisten with light green leaves on sunny spring days, I happened to be given a ride home from Cabra Gallery Museum by George, the director of Gulf Island Film & TV School on Galiano. In making his acquaintance, I discovered that a course I have been interested in was running at the school, and I began to hope I could return to Galiano to study there. A couple of months later, I returned to Rose's to study in the 3D computer animation course, commuting to and from the school while taking care of the pets and volunteering at Cabra Gallery Museum. On Christmas Eve, during my first winter on Galiano, there was a farewell party held for Rose, having hot tea at the table in Andrew's living room, before she left for Nova Scotia. Rose and Andrew talked about his photo in the character Don Quixote, her oil painting promoting the conservation of nature, my hand-drawn Christmas cards and the sense of duty they attributed to their belief and friendship. It was a heartwarming moment that filled with the grace of Christmas. To express my gratitude for the islanders' kindness and the time I had spent with my Island Time host family, Rose and Andrew, I sent an article about my stay on the island, entitled "Ever Green Galiano" to the island's monthly community newsletter, announcing an art show of my drawings worked during the winter at Cabra Gallery Museum. My art show had a few visitors for two weeks in the early spring, as new light green leaves sprouted from the trees, and spring flowers in red, pink, and so on came into blossom. Still, I was happy to give thanks for my stay during the winter. When my Island Time host family and her neighbor visited my art show, I gave them a few prints of my hand-drawn cards by way of thanks. Likewise, I left the prints of all my hand-drawn cards made of my drawings in the museum.

애완 강아지 디니와 봅, 2007년 겨울, 한지, 먹, 22×24Cm²
Dini & Bob, Pets, Winter 2006, Oriental ink, Han(Korean) paper

우정(友情)

　　이따금 섬 거주자의 일부인 야생동물들이 로즈의 뜰을 방문하곤
했다. 뜰에 나타났던 야생동물 중, 사슴은 당당한 눈길로 한동안 나와
눈길을 나누었다. 먹이를 구하여 음식 찌꺼기 처리장 근처에 나타난
라쿤은 나를 보자마자 달아났다. 그와 달리 인간가족의 일부를 이루
는 애완동물은 강자가 약자를 잡아먹는 야생의 법칙이 아니라, 추상
적인 우정, 그리움 등의 개념으로 이해 가능한, 가장 흥미로운 우화
(寓話)의 인물이었다. 목 둘레에 줄을 맨 로즈의 강아지 디니와, 이웃
집의 강아지 봅은 우정에 관해 생각나게 했다. 어느 날, 뜰 음식 처리
장에 디니를 데리고 갔다가 목줄을 놓치자, 숲으로 뛰어 들어 봅이
있는 이웃집으로 달아났다. 나는 뒤좇아 이웃집을 방문하여 인사를
나누고 로즈의 안부를 전했다. 두 강아지는 함께 나란히 걷고, 잔듸
위에서 원을 그려 맴돌았다. 갑자기 디니가 짓으며 봅을 할퀴었지만,
봅은 조용했다. 그것은 야생에서의 싸움 연습같이 보였다. 다음 날
아침, 봅이 우리를 방문했다. 디니 그릇의 가득찬 음식을 다 먹고 거
닐었지만, 디니는 다투지 않았다. 그 관심은 야생동물이 찾는 먹이에
있지 않고, 보다 감성적인 데 있는 듯했다. 내가 다른 애완동물을 쓰
다듬으면 짓으며 날뛰었다. 부재(不在)중인 주인을 그리워 하는 듯,
무엇인가를 찾아 방 안과 산책 길을 두리번 거리고 식욕이 없었다.
뒷뜰 쪽 베란다에서 "너희 우정을 기억하려고 사진을 찍을 건데, 나
란히 서 봐!" 라고 말하며 손짓하였을 때, 두 강아지는 나를 이해하려
는 듯 나란히 정답게 섰다. 내가 섬을 떠날 때, 멀어져 가는 섬에서 로
즈는 디니와 그 같이 나란히 서서 "안녕!" 하고 작별인사를 했다.

Friendship

Once in a while, the wildlife that occupied the island appeared in Rose's yards. Deer would share a stately look with me for a while, but racoons hunting around her compost bin in search of prey would run away as soon as they noticed me. Differently from them, the pets that partly formed of her human family were like those characters in the most interesting allegory, who can be understood in terms of abstract concepts - friendship, longing, and so forth, rather than any natural order, the strong preying on the weak. Watching Rose's dog, Dini on a leash and a neighbouring dog, Bob reminded me of friendship. One day, when I forgot Dini's leash on our way to the compost bin in Rose's garden, he ran away across the woods to the neighbour's house, where Bob lived. I went after him and ran over to the neighbour's, saying hello and passing on Rose's regards. Both dogs were side by side, circling each other on the neighbour's lawn. Then Dini barked loudly and bit Bob, but Bob didn't get angry at all. It seemed like a game they were playing to practise fighting in the wild. The next morning, Bob visited us and ate all the food in Dini's bowl. Then he was sauntering around, yet Dini didn't get angry. Dini's interests seemed to be purely emotional; unlike the foraging wild life, he was not interested in any prey. He would bark jealously and flee wherever he was sitting when the other pets were being stroked. Seemingly owing to longing for Rose, he used to just look around with trembling eyes, without any appetite at home or on our way for a walk. I hand-signaled to both of them telling, "Step side by side on the back deck to take a photo so as to remember your friendship!" They looked like trying to understand me. Rose held Dini on his leash at her side, as they said, "Good Bye!" to me, seemingly in the same way as the two pet dogs had. As I boarded the ferry to leave for my country, Rose and Dini stood on the islands' pier and grew further and further away.

트린코말리 채널, 2006년 겨울, 도화지, 수채물감, 먹, 35×44Cm^2
Trincomali Channel,
Winter 2006, Watercolours & Oriental ink, Drawing paper

녹색 섬

　　페리로부터 멀어져 가는 군도(群島) 속에 보인 그 섬은, 자연 속에서 인간과 동물이 평화롭게 공존하고, 내 희망이 이루어진 따뜻하고 흥미로운 곳이었다. 당시 나는 로즈의 집으로 돌아가 웹 미술관을 다시 열고, 동영상 수업을 들을 계획을 갖고 있었다. 가방에는 토요시장에서 구한 영어로 씌어진 캐나다의 이야기 책, 책장 사이의 말린 나뭇잎, 나의 그림, 섬 사람들의 주소록이 있었다. 서신교환에 의하면, 아일랜드 타임 가족은 벤쿠버의 손자녀들을 돌보기 위해 섬을 떠났다. 로즈는 학업을 마친 후 섬에서 노인 방문치료 자원봉사를 하며, 창작과 신앙연구에 집중하고 있다. 앤드류는 "모든 것이 변함없지만 조금 속도가 느려졌어요!" 라고 했다. 영화학교로부터는 새 학기 개설을 안내하는 전자우편과 페이스북에서의 졸업생들에게 보내는 인사말을 받곤 한다. 세 번째로 캐나다를 방문하여 애드몬튼에서 응급구조과정이 있는 유아와 약자를 돌보는 훈련을 받게 된 동기 중 하나는 나의 섬 거주의 두 번째 해 여름 어느 날 손가락을 다친 사고에서 기인되었다. 그때, 한 이웃의 일본인과 캐나다인 가족이 섬의 유일한 응급실로 데려다 주었다. 그 후 이 가족과 함께 페블 비치에 갔다. 물은 따뜻하고, 사람들은 애완동물과 함께 공 줍기훈련을 하고 있었다. "그 일본인 부인은 섬 공회장에서 캐나다에서의 일본인의 역사강연회를 자원하여 가졌어요!"라고 섬 사람들은 말했다. 섬으로 돌아가기 전 앤드류로부터 "귀양(貴孃)의 글이 실린 섬 소식지가 출판되었어요!" 라고 전해 들었다. 근심하기 보다는 희망을 그렸던 대양(大洋)은 봄 볕에 옅어진 푸른빛으로 반짝였다. "녹색 섬아, 또 봐!" 라고 나는 낮게 말해 보았다.

Island in Green

The island receding from the ferry I was aboard, nestled between the Gulf Islands and Vancouver island, was a warm and interesting place where the wild creatures and humans coexist at peace in nature and my wishes came true. At that time, I had a plan to return to Rose's to take the short course at the film school and to reopen the museum's website. In my bag, I had a few English books of Canadian stories that I had got from Saturday Market, a few dried leaves inserted in the books, my drawings and an addresses book filled with the islanders' detail. My correspondence revealed that my Island Time host family left the island for Vancouver to look after their grandchildren. Rose volunteers her services as a gerontologist on visits to elderly islanders after completing her studies, while remaining dedicated to her art work and religion. Andrew told me, "I am the same as ever, just moving more slowly!" The film school has occasionally informed the alumni of the courses open to us and sent out messages on Facebook. One of the causes that motivated me to thirdly visit Canada in order to take the caregiver's course which includes the first aid training in Edmonton was an accidental injury on my finger in the summer of my second stay on the island; a neighbouring Japanese and Canadian family took me to the emergency room in the only clinic on the island. After that, we went to Pebble Beach together, where the water was very warm and people were enjoying their ball training with their dogs. Some islanders had given me rides told, "The Japanese lady had lectured on the Japanese history in Canada as a volunteer at the community centre!" Before returning to the island, Andrew sent news by e-mail, "The island newsletter with your article was published!" The Strait of Georgia where I had had the hopes rather than worried of the stay for the winter glinted in light blue in the spring sunshine. I murmured, "Island in green, see you again!"

참 조 REFERENCES

1) http://www.uncletomscabin.org/

2) http://www.osblackhistory.com/history.php

3) http://www.civilwarhome.com/commissionreport.htm

4) http://www.chemainus.com/arts/murals/index.htm

5) http://www.chemainus.com/arts/museums.htm

6) http://en.wikipedia.org/wiki/Galiano_Island

7) http://www.galianoconservancy.ca/

8) http://en.wikipedia.org/wiki/Cat

9) http://en.wikipedia.org/wiki/Bird_watching

10) http://galianoisland.com/todo

11) http://www.donquijote.org/vmuseum/

12) http://www.muralact.com

13) http://en.wikipedia.org/wiki/Santa_Claus

14) http://www.thecanadianencyclopedia.com/index.cfm?
PgNm=TCE&Params=A1ARTA0007963

지 도 출 처 MAP RESOURCES

15) http://www.galianoisland.com/maps

16) http://www.bcferries.com/files/images/maps/bcf-
all_routes_map.pdf

 페리 보트 **Ferry Boat,** 2011, Maya

Island Time   http://www.islandtime.freehomepage.com/index.html

갈리아노(Galiano Island)[15]

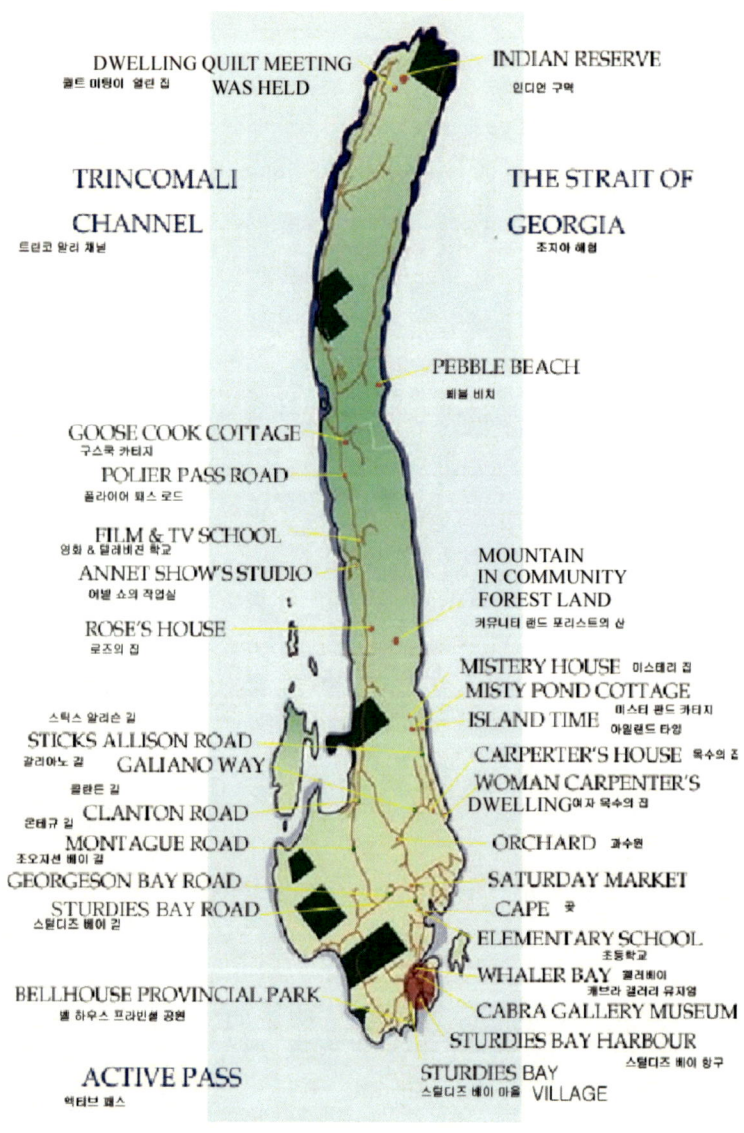

DWELLING QUILT MEETING
퀼트 미팅이 열린 집 WAS HELD

INDIAN RESERVE
인디언 구역

TRINCOMALI
CHANNEL
트린코 말리 채널

THE STRAIT OF
GEORGIA
조지아 해협

PEBBLE BEACH
피블 비치

GOOSE COOK COTTAGE
구스쿡 카티지

POLIER PASS ROAD
폴라이어 패스 로드

FILM & TV SCHOOL
영화 & 텔레비전 학교

ANNET SHOW'S STUDIO
어넷 쇼의 작업실

ROSE'S HOUSE
로즈의 집

MOUNTAIN
IN COMMUNITY
FOREST LAND
커뮤니티 랜드 포리스트의 산

MISTERY HOUSE 미스테리 집
MISTY POND COTTAGE
미스티 팬드 카티지
ISLAND TIME 아일랜드 타임

스틱스 알리슨 길
STICKS ALLISON ROAD
갈리아노 길 GALIANO WAY
클랜튼 길
운테규 길 CLANTON ROAD
MONTAGUE ROAD
조오자선 베이 길
GEORGESON BAY ROAD
STURDIES BAY ROAD
스털디즈 베이 길

CARPERTER'S HOUSE 목수의 집
WOMAN CARPENTER'S
DWELLING 여자 목수의 집

ORCHARD 과수원

SATURDAY MARKET

CAPE 곶

ELEMENTARY SCHOOL
초등학교
WHALER BAY 웰러베이
케브라 갤러리 유지엄
CABRA GALLERY MUSEUM

BELLHOUSE PROVINCIAL PARK
벨 하우스 프라빈셜 공원

STURDIES BAY HARBOUR
스털디즈 베이 항구

ACTIVE PASS
엑티브 패스

STURDIES BAY
스털디즈 베이 마을 VILLAGE

벤쿠버 아일랜드와 걸프 아일랜즈
(Vancouver Island & Gulf Islands)[16]

--- 페리보트 노선 Boat Route